JENNIFER UNDRESSED
IN THE DEEP SHADOWS . . .

Fargo was half under his bedroll as Jennifer lay down a few feet away. He noticed the full swell of her breasts and long legs. He smiled as he saw her slip the small pistol under her blanket and let his voice fill with disappointment.

"You ought to trust people more," he said.

She took a moment to answer. "My, you are sharp-eyed, aren't you?"

"That's what you're paying me for," he reminded her.

"I want to be sure you don't have any wrong ideas," she said from under the blanket. "I've noticed the way you look at a woman."

"I understand," Fargo said. "That's why I've got my Colt right here beside me. Don't think I haven't noticed the way you look at me . . ."

D1599212

Exciting Westerns by Jon Sharpe

THE TRAILSMAN
29

HIGH MOUNTAIN GUNS

by

Jon Sharpe

A SIGNET BOOK

NEW AMERICAN LIBRARY

NAL BOOKS ARE AVAILABLE AT QUANTITY DISCOUNTS
WHEN USED TO PROMOTE PRODUCTS OR SERVICES.
FOR INFORMATION PLEASE WRITE TO PREMIUM MARKETING DIVISION,
NEW AMERICAN LIBRARY, 1633 BROADWAY,
NEW YORK, NEW YORK 10019.

Copyright © 1984 by Jon Sharpe

The first chapter of this book appeared in *Hostage Trail*, the twenty-eighth volume of this series.

SIGNET TRADEMARK REG. U.S. PAT. OFF. AND FOREIGN COUNTRIES
REGISTERED TRADEMARK—MARCA REGISTRADA
HECHO EN CHICAGO, U.S.A.

SIGNET, SIGNET CLASSIC, MENTOR, PLUME, MERIDIAN AND NAL BOOKS
are published by New American Library,
1633 Broadway, New York, New York 10019

First Printing, May, 1984

1 2 3 4 5 6 7 8 9

PRINTED IN THE UNITED STATES OF AMERICA

The Trailsman

Beginnings . . . they bend the tree and they mark the man. Skye Fargo was born when he was eighteen. Terror was his midwife, vengeance his first cry. Killing spawned Skye Fargo, ruthless, cold-blooded murder. Out of the acrid smoke of gunpowder still hanging in the air, he rose, cried out a promise never forgotten.

The Trailsman, they began to call him all across the West, searcher, scout, hunter, the man who could see where others only looked, his skills for hire but not his soul, the man who lived each day to the fullest, yet trailed each tomorrow. Skye Fargo, the Trailsman, the seeker who could take the wildness of a land and the wanting of a woman and make them his own.

*Autumn, 1861, the Colorado Territory,
where the towering Rocky Mountains
waited to swallow the
desperate and the damned . . .*

1

"Get lost, honey," the big man muttered from under the hat that all but covered his face.

"I will definitely not get lost," he heard the young woman snap. Through half-open eyes, he watched her boots, light-brown with fancy stitching. They stayed firmly planted in the soft ground. "I've come a long way to find you, Mr. Fargo," the young woman said.

Fargo's chair tilted back on two legs to rest against the old shack, his hard-packed frame stretched out, feet resting atop an old crate. "Tough," he grunted from under the hat. "Now get lost. I'm resting."

"You're not resting. You're recovering," he heard her spit out. He grunted, not moving. Sharp tongue, he took note, and accurate. He never argued with the truth. It had been a night of good bourbon and good memories with old friends. "I'm staying right here, Mr. Fargo," he heard the young woman say.

"Then stop cackling," Fargo murmured.

"I'm not cackling. I'm trying to talk to you," she flung back.

There was silence from under the hat. Fargo closed his eyes, sighed. He had chosen the spot just outside of town. Sun and silence: one for the body, the other for the head. It had been working out fine, the throbbing in his head growing less, until she had appeared. He heard her fling words at him again.

"Are you going to pay attention to me, dammit?" she said, exasperation holding her voice.

"Not so's you could notice," Fargo murmured. "Get lost, doll."

"A gentleman would at least be courteous," she snapped reprovingly.

"Go find yourself one," Fargo muttered.

"Damn you," Fargo heard her hiss, opened his eyes just wide enough to see the fancy boots spin around. He remained unmoving, chair tilted back against the shack, as her boots disappeared from view, and he heard her climb onto a horse. He closed his eyes, grunted in satisfaction, wondered idly how she had found him in the first place. The throbbing in his head interfered with the acuteness of his usual wild-creature hearing. He caught the faint swish of air too late, pushed the hat up from over his face just as the lariat snapped around the tilted leg of the chair. He had time only for glimpsed impressions, a dark-brown horse, a tan buckskin jacket, long carrot-color hair, and then he was flipping up and backward as the chair went out from under him.

He felt the stab of pain as the back of his head slammed into the old shack and an explosion of yellow lights went off inside his head, and then he was on the ground, being pulled as his left foot caught in the chair. He felt himself being bounced across the ground, dust flying into his face, then wetness as he landed in a puddle of mud and rainwater. His foot came free as the chair went crashing on, yanked along by the lariat, and he lay facedown in the mud puddle.

The horse galloping away reached him as a dim sound. He lay still, let the flashing yellow lights slowly subside in his head. He pushed himself onto one elbow, blew out air, and spit the mud away from his lips. He shook his head, winced, and pushed himself to his feet, his chiseled handsomeness set with anger under the mud that caked his face.

"Goddamn," Fargo said. "Bitch." He looked down

the road that led to town but it was empty. He slowly turned, walked to the magnificent Ovaro standing near, glistening black fore and hind quarters, gleaming white midsection. He pulled himself onto the horse, headed away from town into the low timberland that sprang up almost at once. He found a fast-running brook that babbled its way down from the hills; he slid from the saddle, pulled off clothes, and sank into the cold water. He shivered for a moment but felt the rush of blood rising to his skin, pushed his head into the water, and let the mud and dirt wash away. He pulled his head up, swung from the brook, stretched his powerfully muscled, naked handsomeness in the warmth of the afternoon sun. He let himself dry, then took a bar of hard soap from his saddlebag, knelt beside the brook, and washed the mud from his shirt and trousers. Finished, he spread both pieces on the low branches of a nearby elm to dry, and he lay down again, this time on a soft bank of nut moss growing near the brook.

His lake-blue eyes were still frosted in anger as he thought about the girl. Damn little bitch, he muttered silently. She'd appeared out of nowhere, demanded he talk to her, and now she'd disappeared just as abruptly. She'd hightailed it into town, he wagered. He'd find her, he growled, teach her a lesson. Damned if he'd just let her get away with it. He hadn't much to go on: a tan buckskin jacket and carrot-colored hair. But he'd tracked trails with less to follow. The carrot hair ought to be enough, he mused. Rimrock wasn't that big a town. She was a damn spitfire, that much he'd learned, and he found himself more than angry now. Who was she? he wondered. What the hell had sent her onto him with such determined fury? No ordinary reason, he was certain, and he wondered how she'd come to find him. Willie and Joe, he grunted. They were the only ones who knew he'd headed out of town to nurse his throbbing head.

He felt the faint smile touch his lips. It had been a hell of a night with Willie and Joe, but it had been worth it. He hadn't seen Willie Targel and Joe Kit in years, not since they'd helped him blaze trail through the Texas Territory into Chihuahua, Mexico. They'd been long in the tooth then for that kind of trail riding and had made it their last job. They'd settled in Rimrock to run a harness shop and stable, and he had finally found a run to bring him into Colorado. It had been a time for celebrating and they'd all made the most of it, closed up Rimrock's only saloon and dance hall as dawn approached.

He stretched, tried to see how much of the night he could really remember. Not too much of the last part of it, he grunted. He remembered the girl, younger than the others, remembered putting her off with a promise to return. Girls were easy to come by. Old friends and old memories came all too seldom, so he'd stayed with Willie and Joe and the bourbon bottle. He smiled to himself, closed his eyes, let the sun caress his nakedness. His head had stopped throbbing, and he rose, went to his clothes to find they were dried and warm, dressed, and swung onto the Ovaro. He headed back toward town, not hurrying in the late-afternoon sun.

Rimrock nestled at the edge of the Medicine Bow Range of the great Rocky Mountains. It was a town that drew life from those traveling north and south alongside the mountains. To go west meant crossing directly over the towering peaks, and there were few desperate enough for that. His lake-blue eyes narrowed as he peered into the distance where the great mountains rose up and seemed to touch the sky. They were their own contradiction, these vast mountains, majesty and beauty, power and cruelty, sweepingly awesome in each. Colorado hadn't been a territory for even a year, a land still as untamed as when the Spanish explorers claimed it for themselves and gave it its name, *Colorado*, the red land. They'd called it that after the reddish color of the great Colorado River, and since then the wild land had often been drenched in another kind of red as the Arapaho met the white man's intrusions with fire and arrow.

It remained a place of wild things: rich, fertile, the western half consumed by the great Rocky Mountains and its vast forest ranges, virgin lakes, a land where the moose and the marten, the gray fox and the timber wolf, the eagle and the black-capped chickadee shared the richness of its bounty and the power of its cruelty. Towns seemed out of place in this beauty and wildness, especially those such as Rimrock that clung like fragile leaves in the shadow of the towering peaks. But they clung and made their own oasis and the first wooden buildings came into view as he neared town, as out of place as the mirages seen by a desert traveler.

Fargo headed directly for the center of town and the little harness shop alongside the stable. Willie and Joe were both working on a two-hitch harness as he halted at the doorway, stayed in the saddle. Willie's thin face lifted, looked at him, followed by Joe Kit's parchment countenance.

"Where is she?" Fargo growled.

"Who?" Willie frowned.

"That damned hellcat you sent after me?" Fargo barked.

Both men shrugged. "I see she found you," Joe Kit said.

"She did," Fargo said, bitterness edging his voice. "Why in hell did you send her after me in the first place?"

"She stopped by, said it was real important she talk to you," Willie answered. "Ben at the dance hall sent her to us, she said."

"You get her name?" Fargo questioned.

"She didn't give it," Willie said, peered at Fargo. "She give you trouble?" he asked.

"Real little bitch," Fargo said. "What'd she look like under that carrot top?"

"Pretty, real pretty," Joe Kit said. "Sort of lavender eyes."

Fargo wheeled the pinto. "She comes back, you find out where she's staying," he said, sent the horse into a trot until he reined up in front of Rimrock's only hotel, a gray-white two-story structure with a chipped sign hanging in front that proclaimed itself a *Hostelry*. He snorted at the sign as he went into the small lobby, which sported a frayed carpet and a drooping potted plant. A man looked up from behind the top of a wooden barrier that served as a front desk, thin-faced, watery blue eyes in a face that tried to pull itself into pomposity.

"A girl, orange-reddish hair," Fargo said. "She staying here?"

The man tried to look down his nose as he stared up at the big man. "We don't give out information on our guests," he said stiffly.

Fargo leaned his big hands on the top of the wooden barrier. "You have a doctor in this town?" he asked. The man nodded. "You're going to be his next patient unless you answer me right," Fargo said.

The watery eyes seemed to grow smaller. "It's against the rules," the man said, swallowed hard.

"I just made new rules. You've got three seconds left," Fargo growled. "Orange-red hair, good-looking, I'm told."

The man swallowed again. "She was here," he said. Fargo waited. "She left, about an hour ago," the desk clerk said.

"What room did she have?" Fargo asked.

"Room three, down the hall," the man said.

Fargo strode away, went down the narrow hallway left of the lobby, and found room three. His hand swallowed up the doorknob as he turned it and entered. The room was empty, a lone closet

14

door hanging open. His eyes halted at a small lamp on a round table, a note propped up against it. He crossed the room in two long strides, scooped up the note, scanned the neat writing.

I expected you'd come charging after me like a mad bull. Next time be more courteous. You want to find me, come to Three-way Rock.

"Damn," he muttered as he crumpled the note, tossed it back on the table. He turned, strode from the room, and reached the lobby, halted at the desk clerk. "She had a name," he said.

"Carlyle, Jennifer Carlyle," the man muttered, and Fargo nodded back, strode from the hotel. The gray-purple of dusk had started to settle over the town and he grimaced as he swung onto the Ovaro, sent the horse into a fast canter. He'd seen the rock as he came into town yesterday, standing free halfway up a low hill, a tall boulder that jutted out in three sections, each facing a different direction. He rode with his lips drawn tight. He toyed with the idea of forgetting about her, but curiosity and a lingering anger pushed the thought aside. He'd ridden about a quarter-mile outside of town when he espied the boulder outlined in the fast-gathering dusk, steered the Ovaro toward it. His hand rested on the big Colt .45 on his hip as he neared the unusual boulder, and his eyes swept the brush on three sides of it. Nothing moved and he felt his black brows knitting as he halted in front of the rock. He stayed still in the saddle as he peered at the rock. The three sections afforded plenty of places to stay out of sight, and he saw narrow crevices running inside the three arms of the boulder.

"I'd hide, too, if I were you, honey," he said.

The voice answered after a moment. "I'm not hiding. I'm watching," it said. His eyes snapped to the section of the rock that faced north. "Don't you

15

move, Mr. Fargo," she said. "There's a big Spencer pointed at you."

"I'm real scared," Fargo said. His eyes stayed riveted on the rock and he caught the movement, half-hidden in the darkening shadows of the boulder. She stepped forward, the rifle in her hands, moved toward him, came out of the shadows.

Joe Kit hadn't been wrong. She was more than pretty: shoulder-length carrot-colored hair framing a strikingly attractive face; lovely, full lips; a short, slightly turned-up nose; and eyes the color of sweet-violet. The tan buckskin jacket hung open enough to let him see high, full breasts under the white shirt. The fancy riding boots ended long, full-thighed legs that were planted slightly apart, a pose more provocative than she realized, he was certain.

"You come ready to listen?" she said.

"I've come to fan your little ass," Fargo growled, swung down from the Ovaro.

"We'll both be sorry if you try that," she said. His eyes questioned further. "You'll be holding a bullet in your gut and I'll be out one trailsman."

His lake-blue eyes studied her. The rifle didn't waver and her sweet-violet eyes stayed steady. The lovely line of her jaw held strength and determination in it. "Jennifer Carlyle," he said, his eyes narrowed.

"That's right," she said. "You ready to listen now?"

He let his lips purse for a moment, gave a little half-shrug. "Why not?" he said. "You sure have something sticking hard in you." He tossed her a smile, saw her take in the powerfulness of his body, the handsome chiseled strength of his face. "Only I don't listen well with a gun pointing at me. Bothers my concentration," he said.

"All right," she said, lowered the big Spencer.

Fargo's arms shot out with the speed of a cougar's spring, one hand closing around the rifle, tearing it from her, the other hand around her arm, spinning her, yanking her to him.

"Bastard," he heard her scream as he tossed the rifle aside, dropped to one knee, and flipped her onto her stomach. He lifted her skirt, saw pink bloomers covering a beautifully rounded rear. His hand came down hard and she screamed, tried to twist and kick, but his other hand held her down across the back of her neck. He slammed down on the soft rear again, stopped counting after ten strokes. She cursed and screamed, and he heard her sobs as he gave her a final smack, stood up, and let her fall to the ground. Her sobs were made as much of fury as of pain as she rolled away from him, got to one knee, the sweet-violet eyes shooting blue-lavender flame.

"You rotten, lying no-good bastard," she flung at him.

"Now I'll listen," he said almost affably.

"You goddamn lying bastard. I've got nothing to say to you," she spit out as she got to her feet, one hand rubbing her rear.

He shrugged, picked up the Spencer, removed the shells, and tossed the rifle onto the ground as he walked to the Ovaro. He had one leg up in the stirrup as he heard her half-strangled cry. "Wait, goddamn you," she called. He took his foot from the stirrup, glanced back at her, watched the fury blaze in her eyes as her lovely lips twitched.

"You going to talk or waste time arguing with yourself?" he asked impatiently. He saw the glower replace fury, noted that she was as attractive angry as she was quiet.

"I need you," she spit at him. "I need you, and that's the only damn reason I'm going to talk to you."

He smiled. "Good reason, that," he approved. "Talk."

2

The sweet-violet eyes had grown darker, almost a purple, and anger still simmered behind the words she clipped out. "You're the very best, I was told. They call you the Trailsman. That's why I came looking for you," she said.

"Who told you I'd be here?" Fargo asked.

"Herb Landower back in Cheyenne Wells," she answered. "I want you to find someone, a man. I want him found dead or alive. His name's Jack Slattery."

"He run out on you?" Fargo queried with a half-smile.

"No," she flared. "Jack Slattery ran out with my daddy's life savings. A month ago he ran off and Daddy died of a heart attack because of it. I want Jack Slattery and the money he took."

"I take it you've some idea which way he headed," Fargo said.

"I've a sort-of map," Jennifer Carlyle said, and he picked up the tiny note of apology in her tone.

"What's that mean?" he asked.

"It marks places and cabins. I guess he'd gone from one to the other, and maybe that makes it sort of a map," she said. "It's something to go on," she added defensively.

"Something," he conceded. "No map, even the best of them, is much when it comes to breaking trail. How come you have this sort-of map?"

She drew a deep breath, leaned back against the

tall boulder, and he enjoyed how her breasts pushed the buckskin jacket open with their fullness. "Jack Slattery talked my daddy into a business partnership Slattery was a mapmaker. He figured there'd be a lot of maps needed out here in a new territory, and he got my daddy to finance him," she explained. "Slattery had a strange habit. He always drew two of every map he made. When he ran out, he left in a hurry and forgot the second map he'd drawn for himself. I found it going through the house."

"Where is it?" Fargo asked.

"You can see it when the time comes, when I'm sure about you helping me," she said, and he saw anger come into her eyes again. "You tricked me before and I don't trust people who trick me," she said.

"You bushwhacked me with that lariat. I don't trust people who do that," Fargo said blandly.

She glowered. "You wouldn't pay attention to me," she said.

"Tell me the rest before I stop paying attention again," Fargo said.

"I'm prepared to pay you very well," she said with sudden stiffness.

"How well?" he asked.

"A thousand dollars. Half now, the rest when you find him," Jennifer said.

Fargo let his brows lift. "A lot of money," he agreed. "Especially since this Slattery ran off with everything."

"This is money I saved," she said quickly, almost too quickly.

He studied her, let thoughts lie quietly inside him, nothing formed but little stirrings that pushed at him. "Slattery must've stolen a bundle," he commented.

"It was a lot of money," she conceded.

Fargo kept his voice bland. "What'd your pa do before he hooked up with this Slattery?" he asked.

"He drove for a haulage outfit back in Kansas," she said.

Fargo nodded, filed the reply in with his unformed thoughts. "Where do you aim to chase this Slattery?" he asked, and saw Jennifer's lips draw tight for a moment in the dusk.

She turned abruptly, the orange-red hair swirling, her eyes trained on the purple-gray towering peaks beyond Three-way Rock. "Up there," she said. "High up into the Rockies. That's where he's gone." She turned back to look at the big man and saw the disbelief gathering in his lake-blue eyes.

"Honey, you're either plumb stupid or plumb crazy," Fargo said.

She drew indignation around her at once. "I'm neither. If he can go there, you certainly ought to be able to take me after him," she said.

Fargo made a derisive sound. "Not now," he grunted.

"What does that mean?" She frowned.

"You said he has a month's start. That's enough to make the difference," Fargo told her.

"Difference?" she echoed.

"Spelled time, honey, t-i-m-e. Look up at those mountains. There's just enough high sun up there left. What do you see?"

"Mountains, trees, foliage," Jennifer Carlyle said, staring at the tall peaks.

"Foliage," Fargo repeated. "Not green foliage."

"No, it's turning color—reds, yellows, fall trees," Jennifer said.

"That means the snows can come anytime now up in high mountain country, snows that come on winds you can't stand up to, snows that freeze and blanket everything, fill passes so not even a field mouse can get through, the Snows That Kill, the Indians call them." He paused, watched her eyes stare at him, round lavender orbs. "It means you're out of time, honey. It means that if the Arapaho don't get you and the mountains don't break you, the snows will kill you once and for all."

"I understand the Indians live out the winter in the mountains. So do some trappers," she said.

"The Indians come down to the foothills and they prepare for the winter. A trapper who wants to hole up spends all summer getting ready. You wouldn't last longer than a mayfly up there."

"Maybe the snows will be late this year. It's possible. You can't say differently for sure," she threw back.

"No, I can't," he conceded.

"I'm going. I want Slattery," she said. "I'll take the chance."

"Good luck," he commented.

"You saying you won't ride trail for me?" she pressed.

"Give the lady a cigar," Fargo returned.

Jennifer Carlyle turned from him, pulled herself onto the dark-brown horse, her carrot-colored hair swinging angrily in the last of the daylight. She looked down at him, the sweet-violet eyes dark with contempt. "I see I made a mistake looking for you. They didn't tell me you were so lily-livered," she slid at him.

"Lily-livered's one thing. Being a damn fool's another," Fargo said calmly, turned, and swung onto the Ovaro. "I'll ride back to the hotel with you," he said.

"I don't need the Trailsman to find my way back there," she said, coating each word with sarcasm.

He swung the Ovaro beside her, ignored her remark, rode with her back to town in silence.

She dismounted when they reached the hotel, cast a narrowed glance up at him. "What if I doubled the pay?" she asked.

His smile held more than she realized as he added the offer to the unformed reservations that pushed

21

at him. "More money won't change the mountains. More money won't buy time," he answered.

"Sometimes it gives a man backbone," she snapped.

"And gives a woman more damn-fool notions," he growled. "Go home. Wait till spring to track Slattery," he said gruffly.

"No," she snapped. "I'll find someone not so timid to ride trail for me."

"If you don't?" Fargo asked.

"I'll go on by myself. I'm not afraid," she said.

"Fools never are," he grunted.

She threw an angry glance at him and stalked into the hotel, paused in the doorway to look back. "I'll be here till tomorrow, if you find enough courage," she said. "Double the pay, remember."

"I'll remember," he said, watched her disappear inside the house. He turned the Ovaro, slowly headed down the street toward the dance hall. She was being a damn fool, but something was driving her to it, he mused. She'd given him a story smooth enough to satisfy most people. But his life was made of looking for signs, reading trails, detecting the false leads from the real ones. Her story didn't satisfy him. Little things, not enough to be sure of but enough to wonder about. She wasn't going to give up, he was certain of that much. A damn waste, he muttered inwardly, a young woman that good-looking getting herself killed. The money she offered wasn't easy to turn down, and his hand lifted, pressed against the letter in the inside pocket of his jacket. But, damn, he wasn't about to make it a double suicide. He frowned. Maybe she'd come to her senses and take his advice, he pondered and heard himself grunt derisively at the thought. No chance in hell for that. She was too bent on going after Slattery, too determined, Fargo told himself. That determination was one of the little things that stuck inside him.

He pushed further speculation about Jennifer Carlyle aside as he reached the dance hall, dropped the

Ovaro's reins over the hitching post, and went inside the big, square room. The brightness and noise assaulted him at once, and tobacco and cheap perfume mingled together to create that particular odor special to dance halls and saloons. He scanned the tables: Joe and Willie hadn't arrived yet. He sat down at an empty table, ordered a bourbon, and was sipping it as he saw the girl walk toward him. She slid into one of the empty chairs and he remembered her in a veiled sort of way, younger than the others, pretty in a slightly vacant way.

"You kept your promise." She smiled.

"What promise?" he asked warily.

"To come back and see me tonight," she said with a touch of pride.

"That one," he said, and held a sigh of relief inside himself. "Later, honey," he added tersely, sipped on the bourbon.

She hesitated a moment, saw there was no change in his eyes, and rose, walked on without a word, used to being taken or dismissed with the same abruptness.

Fargo sat back, finished the bourbon, and felt the small frown dig into his forehead. It wasn't like Joe or Willie to be this late. He ordered another drink, nursed it, watched the girls work on potential customers. Willie and Joe still hadn't shown as he neared the end of the second drink. He rose, left the glass unfinished, and strode out of the dance hall.

Outside, he led the Ovaro down the street to the harness shop. A dim light shone through the open crack of the almost closed door, and he called out, waited, received no answer. He pushed the door open wider. The shop was still as a tomb and he felt the hairs on the back of his neck begin to stand straight. The lamp hanging on the wall afforded the only light, the back of the harness shop in dark shadows. Something was wrong. He felt the stab of alarm in the pit of his stomach.

Fargo stepped into the shop, one hand on the butt of the Colt in its holster. The rows of harnesses hanging on the walls cast long, wavy-fingered shadows in the dim lamplight. A long wooden workbench took up the center of the room, and he stepped around it, froze as he saw Willie Targel lying facedown on the floor. "Jesus," he hissed as he dropped to one knee and saw Joe Kit's form only a few feet away, also facedown on the floor. He leaned his face down to Willie, heard the man's shallow breathing, and saw the red bruise alongside his temple. He started to move to Joe Kit when he heard the voice cut into his frowning thoughts.

"Don't move, mister," it said.

Fargo stayed motionless, glanced up to see the figure emerge from the shadows, two more coming up behind him. The first man held a Remington six-gun pointed at him, a tall man with a long, sour face. The man to his right sported a blond mustache on a younger face with hard eyes. The third man peered out of a totally ordinary face. "Drop your gun, nice and slow," the tall, sour-faced man ordered.

Fargo eyed the man's revolver. It held steady and was too close for a miss. Cursing silently, he lifted his own Colt .45 out of the holster and let it drop to the floor. The mustached one stepped forward, kicked it away first, then picked it up and shoved it into his belt. The sour-faced man offered a caricature of a smile. "We heard how fast you were, mister," he said. "We figured this was the best way to get the drop on you. Worked real well, too."

Fargo nodded, stared at the man from one knee, and saw the other two move out to half-circle him, one coming up behind him. He felt more than heard the one behind him bring his arm up and down in a chopping motion, tried to dive aside, but the gun barrel caught him alongside the temple. He fell forward, the room suddenly spinning. He shook his

24

head and the room stopped its spinning, and he heard the voice clearly.

"The Carlyle girl wants you to help her. We're gonna make sure you don't do that," it said.

Fargo saw the boot coming at his face out of his peripheral vision. He threw himself sideways and felt the boot graze his cheek. He rolled, tried to regain his feet, but the third man landed on his back, one arm circling his neck, squeezing and pulling his head upward. Fargo let himself go limp and the man slipped, suddenly off balance. His grip loosened for only an instant, but an instant was enough for Fargo. He drove his elbow backward into the man's solar plexus and heard the gasped hiss of pain as the figure fell from him, rolled onto the ground with both hands clasped to his midsection. Fargo saw the tall man and the other one rushing at him, getting in each other's way in the narrow space beside the workbench, and he caught an ankle as he dived forward low, twisted, and the man yelped in pain as he fell. Fargo got an arm up, parried a blow from the hollow-eyed man, started to fire his own looping right when his legs were seized from behind and he fell forward, the blow missing.

The Trailsman took a hard, chopping blow to the back of the neck from the tall man, sprawled forward, and grunted in pain; he tried to get to his feet, but arms circled him from behind. He managed to half-way regain his footing despite the man clinging to him when the tall assailant bulled him into the wall. His face smashed against a harness hanging there, the leather acting as a makeshift cushion, but he felt the breath driven from him as two blows smashed into his kidneys from behind.

"Beat the bastard into the wall," he heard one of his assailants snarl. Fargo steeled his muscles as another blow smashed into his back, got one arm up, yanked the harness from the wall, and flung it around behind him, whiplike.

25

"Ow, goddamn," he heard someone yell.

Fargo whirled, the harness still in his hand. The hollow-eyed man drove a blow at him and he pulled his head aside just in time to miss the full force of it. He flung the harness over the man's head, yanked hard on the leather straps, tightening them, twisting as he pulled. He put his powerful shoulders into a tremendous twisting pull and heard the man's neck snap as his head was all but swiveled completely around. The man crumpled, the harness still around his head, as if he were some grotesque parody of a horse, but Fargo was pulling back again as the second assailant came at him with a roundhouse right.

The man tried to follow through with another, but Fargo ducked, drove a short, hard right upward that cracked against his assailant's jaw. The man staggered backward, seemed about to fall, and Fargo stepped forward, saw the flash of metal as the man drew a bowie knife from his belt. He lunged with it, bringing it down in a sharp arc, and Fargo ducked away, brought his foot out as the man flew past him. The figure stumbled, fell forward, and Fargo heard the guttural gasp of pain. "Aaarrrgh . . . ah, jeez," the figure cried out, rolled over, and the bowie knife jutted from the man's belly.

Fargo whirled, saw the third man struggle to his feet, one hand still clutching his solar plexus, his face contorted with fury and pain, his other hand drawing the gun from its holster. Fargo flung himself sideways as the bullet smashed into the spot where the harness had hung. The man fired again, another wild shot as Fargo rolled against the figure of the tall man. He reached out, found the man's holster, yanked the gun from it as the third man started to come forward to fire again. Fargo's shot caught him full in the chest. The man staggered, his hand still clutching his solar plexus suddenly turning red. He took another two steps, tried to raise the gun. Fargo's finger tightened on the trigger and the

26

gun blasted another shot. The figure seemed to come apart as it crumpled to the floor.

Fargo rose, dropped the gun, and retrieved his own Colt. He leaned against the wall, let his own harsh breathing subside. He saw Joe Kit stir, start to come awake, and Fargo dropped to one knee beside him, helped the man to sit up. Joe Kit's parchment face grimaced as he scanned the room, his eyes returning to the big man at his side. "You, too, eh?" Joe Kit spit out as he saw the red welt along Fargo's temple. A sound came from Willie as he, too, stirred, pushed himself up to a sitting position. He blinked, focused on Fargo after a glance at the three still forms on the floor.

"You got them. Good," he muttered.

"Who are they?" Fargo asked.

"Never saw them before, Fargo," Joe Kit answered. "They came in, asked if we expected you'd be stopping by."

"And I told them we were meeting you at the dance hall," Willie said. "Next thing they belted Joe and me."

"Then sat back and waited for me to come looking for you when you didn't show," Fargo said. "It damn near worked for them. They must have been watching and saw us together last night."

"Why, dammit?" Joe Kit asked, pulling himself slowly to his feet, lending Willie a hand along the way. "What made them come after you, Fargo?"

"One said something about making sure I didn't help Jennifer Carlyle," Fargo said. "She tried to hire me to chase someone up into the mountains."

Joe Kit's brows lifted in thought and he nodded. "Makes some sense, now," he muttered, cast a questioning glance at the big man beside him. "Pretty damn chancy goin' up into the high mountains now," he remarked.

Fargo nodded agreement and saw the slow smile touch the parchment face.

"She payin' good money?" Joe asked.

"Real good," Fargo said.

"You'll take her," Joe Kit said.

"You're pretty sure about what I'll do, you old sodbuster," Fargo returned.

"Can't see you turning down good money and good looks," Joe replied, and chortled at himself.

"Let's get these varmints out of here and go have that drink," Fargo said. "I could use one now."

Willie started for the door. "I'll go get Hamden. He's our gravedigger. Town pays him two dollars a head for everyone he puts under," Willie said. "He'll be happy as a pig in mud when I tell him I've got three for him."

Fargo went through the pockets of the trio as Willie hurried outside; he found none had anything that told him who they were, and when Willie returned, he watched the gravedigger cart them away, a frown touching his forehead. Come morning, he'd learn a little more about Jennifer Carlyle, he decided as he returned to the dance hall with Joe and Willie. They made the night a time for quiet reminiscing, everyone still carrying the night before.

"You'll be riding out tomorrow," Willie said. "Don't wait so long to come this way again."

."I'll try not to," Fargo said. "It's been good seeing you, real good." He hadn't need to say more. Between old friends, words could be just so much extra baggage, and the midnight moon, almost full, hung in the black velvet sky as Fargo rode from Rimrock and found a spot to bed down. The night carried the fall in it, turned chilly, and he made a small fire. His eyes peered across the darkness to where the towering mountain peaks were great black forms against the night sky. He reached into his pocket and drew out the letter. It had caught up to him before he'd left for the Colorado Territory, and he leaned forward closer to the firelight to read it again.

Fargo . . .

It was good hearing from you. You asked how I am. Truth is not good. Not many men want a widow with two young-uns, specially one getting gray in head. It's been tough ever since Jack died, and now it's gone real bad.

I just found out that Jack had never staked a proper claim to the land. A man named Swanson has staked claim to it. If I want the land, I have to pay him five hundred dollars in two months or he takes over and I pack up and go. Five hundred dollars, Fargo. There's just no place I'm going to get that money.

The bank in Belleville turned me down for a loan. They said I couldn't work the land enough to pay it back. Anyway I don't think they'd give a woman a loan, specially a widow with kids. So I guess we'll be moving off after all these years. I don't know to what or to where. You hear of somebody that wants to loan money, you tell him about me. Meanwhile, you keep taking care of yourself, Fargo.

Abby Dunkirk

Fargo folded the letter back into his pocket and his lake-blue eyes stared into the dark. He owed Abby, for herself and for Jack. They had helped him get himself together after his family had been murdered. His thoughts turned Jennifer Carlyle's offer in his mind. The five hundred would mean everything to Abby and not that much to him. Two months, he muttered, the letter blazing inside him. It'd take a month for the money to reach her by post. Abby was near out of time already. Taking Jennifer Carlyle's offer would let him get the money to her in time.

He lay back, pulled the blanket over himself, let thoughts continue to turn inside him. Maybe there was a way to help Abby Dunkirk and keep his own neck in one piece. He'd see about that, come morning, he decided, and he closed his eyes and pushed away further speculation. The day would come soon enough. He slept, the night quiet, no unwelcome sounds to snap him awake, and he let himself sleep later than he usually did, woke with the sun fully over the horizon.

He rose, washed with water from his canteen, dressed, rode slowly back into town. Willie and Joe were hard at work in the shop and didn't see him pass by. He reached the gray-white hotel just as Jennifer Carlyle stepped from the door. The morning sun caught the carrot-color hair to send orange shafts gleaming from it. A pale-green shirt pressed smoothly over her breasts, round, full-curved contours, and without the tan buckskin jacket her waist narrowed quickly into full, well-rounded hips. The sweet-violet eyes, a striking blue-lavender, saw him with a touch of surprise.

"Leaving so early?" Fargo asked as he swung from the Ovaro.

"I was going to the dance hall to post a note on the wall," she said.

"For someone to ride trail for you?" he asked.

"That's right," she snapped. "Or have you changed your mind?"

"Three sidewinders tried to kill me last night," Fargo said. "So I wouldn't help you, they told me. Who were they?"

The violet orbs widened in surprise. "I don't know," she said.

"Hell you don't," he snapped.

Her eyes hardened and her jaw lifted. "I don't," she insisted.

"Who else knows what Slattery ran off with?" Fargo asked.

"I don't know. I didn't tell anybody," she said. "Maybe he did."

"A man running off doesn't go around telling folks," Fargo said.

"I don't know anything," she insisted again. Her eyes didn't waver, he noted. Either she was telling the truth or she was a damn good actress, he muttered inwardly, and didn't discount the latter. He knew only one thing. It was getting harder to buy her story about Slattery and her pa. But he'd wait on that. He saw her studying him. "You didn't answer my question. You change your mind?" she pushed at him.

"That depends, and not for any reasons you'll be thinking," he answered.

"Depends on what?" Jennifer shot back.

"On your getting certain things straight," he said. "You're paying me to ride trail for you, I call the shots. I say where, how, and when we go. If I say it's time to turn back, we turn back. No arguments, no tricks, no second guesses."

"Not that. I'll decide that," Jennifer said. "You can have your say on the trail but not on that." Her chin raised defiantly, her eyes staying on him.

Fargo grimaced. Abby's letter glowed in his pocket, but he had to make Jennifer Carlyle bend first. "Good luck, honey," he said, pulled himself onto the Ovaro, and started to wheel the horse away.

"Wait," he heard her call. He paused, looked back at her. Her face stayed cool, tight, beautifully contained. "If that time comes, we'll decide on it together," she said.

Fargo let his lips purse in thought, but he smiled inwardly. She'd offered a compromise, done the bending. It would do for now. When the time came, there'd be no compromise, he was certain. "All right, you've got a deal. Half now, half later," he said.

"Wait here," she replied, and disappeared into the hotel to return in minutes, the money wrapped in a small sack. "I want to get started at once," she said as he took the money. "We've a good part of the day left. I'll be waiting at the end of town in half an hour."

He nodded. "Maybe you'll be able to come up with something about those sidewinders by then," he said.

The lavender eyes flared at once. "I told you, I can't think who or why," she said.

"Think harder," he tossed back as he rode away. He found the post box was in the sheriff's office, bought a small mail pouch, and sealed the sack of bills inside it. A sign on the wall told him the post rider was scheduled to arrive the following week, and he put the pouch into the mail-drop box. Finished, he rode from town to find Jennifer waiting, sitting on her dark-brown horse, a packhorse beside her. He halted, dismounted, stared at the full loaded animal.

"Where'd you get him?" he asked.

"Brought him with me," she said.

"No good. Wrong horse for the job," Fargo grunted.

"Nonsense. He's a great packhorse. Didn't give me a bit of trouble the whole trip here," Jennifer said.

"Mostly flat country, a few low hills. Where we're going you need a quarter horse, a cutting pony, or better yet, a mule," Fargo said.

"He'll make it fine. I'm not wasting time to go find a packhorse that suits you," Jennifer snapped.

Fargo shrugged. "He won't make it," he repeated, and moved the Ovaro forward to head into the foothills. He rode slowly, ignored the impatience that bristled from Jennifer without words. But he enjoyed watching the way her breasts moved in unison under the lime-green shirt, swaying as one, bouncing as one. Good, firm muscles under the curved loveliness, he grunted.

But the foothills came to an end too quickly, by the late afternoon, and he halted to gaze up at the awesome splendor of the giant mountains. They were clothed in nature's version of Joseph's coat of many colors: brilliant yellows, pale yellows, scarlet and russet, brown and magenta, bright reds and subdued reds, everything a vast expanse of shimmering tones. The colors were still holding their brilliance, a good sign, and he gave thanks for small favors. He turned to Jennifer and observed that her carrot-colored hair fitted in well with the fall foliage.

"Where's that sort-of map. Which way do we head?" he asked.

She fished into a small leather pouch, brought out a folded sheet of paper, and handed it to him. He unfolded it, scanned the sheet, his mouth drawing in unhappily. *Sort-of map* was indeed the correct term for it, the paper setting out a primitive trail marked more by instructions, signposts, and checkpoints than by routes, everything dotted in an irregular pattern. Slattery had made the chart for himself, more as a reminder than a map.

Fargo focused on the first words printed in small letters at the bottom of the sheet with an arrow that pointed northward into the mountains.

"Follow high run of Maples," he read aloud, and let his eyes slowly move up the mountain of dancing colors. "Birches there to the right," he muttered. "Mountain ash next to them. Oaks all through that middle section with some cottonwoods and sycamores mixed in."

Jennifer frowned at him. "How can you tell what kind of trees they are from here?" she asked. "You can't even make out the leaves, much less the shape of them."

"That's one thing good about the fall. I don't have to see anything but the color. Birches turn orange and deep yellow. Ash turn purple-red, oaks turn brown and rust, sycamores medium yellow edged with dull red, cottonwoods a quiet yellow," he told her. "Each kind of tree turns its own color every fall. It never changes." His gaze continued to move up the mountainside, suddenly halted. "Over there to the right, that long line of scarlet and deep yellow,

33

those are maples," he said, let his eyes follow the trees. They mounted high into the mountain, stretched as far as the eye could see. "That's us," he said, and turned the pinto toward the high line of distant trees. "We won't make them till morning," he said.

"You think we can pick up his trail then?" Jennifer asked.

"Can't much pick up a trail over a month old, not in these mountains. Best we can do is pick up signs and hope they're his. There'll be a good chance they'll be that. There's not a hell of a lot of traffic up that way," he said wryly. He led the way upward, watched Jennifer's horse fight hard to keep footing on a suddenly sharp rise, and saw the packhorse slip, fall to its knees twice, just manage to make it to the top of the rise. He rested for a moment to let the packhorse regain its breath.

He saw Jennifer's sweet-violet eyes sparked with defensiveness as she watched him eye the packhorse. "He made it," she said.

"There'll be a hundred like that one, and worse," Fargo said as he led the way forward again. The scarlet-leafed maples were growing closer when the day began to slide away and Fargo halted at a flat spot that let him look out across the mountainside. The great peaks above beckoned endlessly. He scanned down the slope they had come so far, let his eyes move slowly across the terrain. It was the third time he had halted to scan the slope and he lingered a few moments longer before moving on. As he turned the Ovaro upward again, his lake-blue eyes were narrowed and a tight little smile edged the corners of his lips. He found a mountain stream just as the night began to close in, steered the horse to a little glen that flattened out near the stream. He dismounted, Jennifer hitching the packhorse to a low branch; he made a fire as the night brought the sharpness of mountain wind. She unpacked a skillet and a tin of hash from the packhorse, and he built the fire up, watched her kneel down, warm herself for a moment. The carrot hair shot out shafts of copper in the firelight's gleam as she took the skillet, poured the hash into it. She was suddenly very domestic and very beautiful, skillet and sensuousness all wrapped up together.

"Cook slow," he muttered as he moved back into the deeper shadows away from the fire. She glanced up questioningly. "We've been tailed since we left town," he said matter-of-factly, and saw her lovely mouth drop open, her eyes grow wide.

"Are you sure?" she asked.

"Sure as you're holding that skillet," he said. "Seems somebody's been watching your every move, honey." Her frown deepened as she stared at him. "And you've no idea who or why," he said blandly.

"That's right," Jennifer snapped. "I wish you'd stop doubting me."

"I'll try," Fargo said dryly. "Meanwhile, you keep cooking real slow till I get back."

"Where are you going?" she asked, alarm in her voice.

"To get some answers," he said, faded into the blackness before she could voice the protest in her face. He moved through the thick wooded slope with long, loping strides. When he'd first detected they were being followed, he'd made sure to leave an easy trail. The man wouldn't hang back far, he was certain. He'd made camp within sight of the fire, and Fargo moved down the slope silent as a great mountain cat, moving from tree to tree in quick, short, darting steps, sometimes grasping low branches to almost swing forward between the trees.

The half-moon beamed a pale light onto the mountainside, just enough for him to see, when he'd moved a hundred yards or so down the slope, the figure leaning against a tree. He dropped to one knee, watched for a few moments. The figure didn't move, and he edged a few steps closer until he caught the sound of the man's even, shallow breathing. He unholstered the big Colt .45, took two long strides forward, flinging aside stealth, and was before the figure. The man's eyes snapped open and he reached for his gun, froze as the barrel of the big Colt rested against his forehead.

"Try it and your head comes off," Fargo growled.

The man's hand fell to his side and Fargo saw fear in eyes that were set in a round, almost pudgy face. Fargo took the man's gun from his holster, flung it into the blackness of the underbrush. He pulled the Colt back from the pudgy face, took a step backward. "You've been tailing us. Why?" Fargo questioned, his voice hard. He saw bravado push the fear from the man's eyes.

"You're all wrong, mister," the man said, managing to sound aggrieved.

Fargo reached down, seized the man by the front of his jacket, and lifted him to his feet as though he were a rag doll. He spun the man around and slammed him against the tree, and the man cursed in pain as Fargo let go of him, watched him slide to the ground. The man turned slowly and his pudgy face trickled blood from a half-dozen bark-scraped places.

"Answers, no games," Fargo barked.

The man wiped a sleeve across his face and his eyes were still clinging to bravado as he pushed himself to his feet, leaned against the tree. "You're all wrong, partner," he tried again, flinched, tried to draw away as Fargo's blow shot forward, a short, straight right to the belly. "Agh, Christ," he gasped in pain as he fell to his knees, his hand held to his midsection.

"You want to do it the hard way?" Fargo said. "That's fine with me." He seized the man by the shoulder, started to yank him up.

"No, shit, no more," the man breathed, his hand still clutching his belly. Fargo flung him back and the pudgy face looked up at him with pain and fear. The man's words came hard, laced with pain. "He hired me to tail you and the girl," he said.

"Who?" Fargo barked.

"Davis, said his name was Davis," the man answered. "I was to hang back, leave signs, a clear trail to follow."

"Who's this Davis?" Fargo questioned.

"I don't know, honest I don't," the man said, color returning to his pudgy face. "All I know about him is the color of his money."

"How come he found you?" Fargo pressed.

"He heard I'd done some trail riding," the man said. "But I don't know anything else about him. I never saw him before he hired me."

Fargo's gaze bored into the man. There was still fear in the pudgy face. It was just possible he was telling the truth. He'd let it stand at that, Fargo decided and moved to the man's horse, undid the latigo and slid it from the cinch ring, and pulled the saddle free and let it fall to the ground. A sharp slap on the rump sent the horse galloping into the night.

"What the hell are you doing?" the man protested, getting to his feet.

"I'll leave the saddle for you. Start walking. I figure you can make it back to Rimrock in a few days," Fargo said.

"You can't leave me up here without a gun or a horse," the man said.

Fargo's eyes grew hard at once. "I'm leaving you alive. Don't push your luck," he growled. The man's gun was beyond finding in the blackness of the underbrush. "Walk," he said. "Tell this Davis that he's a dead man if he comes after me." He watched the man throw an angry glance as he picked up the saddle and began to trudge away.

Fargo turned and slowly started back up the slope. He'd gone but a half-dozen yards when the shot exploded the night. He felt the searing heat of the bullet as his hat flew from his head. He let himself crumple to the ground, lay on his side, motionless. Through slitted eyes he saw the boots approaching and he cursed at himself. The man had had another gun in his saddlebag, Fargo swore silently at himself. Carelessness on his part. Inexcusable. He saw the figure halt, the man raise his hand to fire another shot.

Fargo flung himself sideways in a half-roll, heard the shot explode and the bullet dig into the ground beside him. But the big Colt was in his hand and he fired from an almost prone position. The pudgy face standing above him disintegrated in a shower of flesh, bone, and redness that momentarily obscured the half-moon.

Fargo pushed himself to his feet to stare at the faceless form lying on the ground. He turned away slowly, began the climb back up the slope toward the flickering light. When he reached the fire, Jennifer stepped from the shadows, the Spencer in her hands, her eyes wide. He saw the relief flood her face.

"Thank God. I heard the shots. I didn't know what to think," she said.

Fargo's eyes were hard. "Who's Davis?" he snapped.

Jennifer frowned. "Davis? I don't know anything about any Davis," she said.

"He knows about you," Fargo said, and told her what had happened with the man. He watched her lovely face for some flicker, a moment's hesitation, a fleeting expression that might reveal something. But there was nothing.

"I don't know any Davis," she said again.

Fargo's eyes continued to study her. Maybe she was telling the truth, he wondered, even though her story was full of things that didn't fit right. Maybe truth was a thing of bits and pieces with her. He'd wait some yet, he decided. There was time.

"You want to change that rifle for that skillet," he said.

She set the gun down and walked to the fire, picked up the skillet, stirred it, emptied it onto a tin plate for him. "It's a little burnt," she said.

"It'll do," he said, ate quickly, and put the fire out with a few handfuls of dirt.

Jennifer undressed in the deep shadows, returned in a nightdress of deep-green cotton that hung to the ground but let a square neckline reveal the full swell of deep breasts, smooth skin that began to turn white at the lower edge of the neckline.

He began to undress to his shorts and she looked away, took out her own blanket as he got his bedroll. He was half under his bedroll as she lay down, and he smiled as he saw her slip the small pistol under her blanket. Foreign-made, he guessed, that kind usually were. Small but deadly enough at close range. He stretched out, gave a deep sigh that easily carried to where she lay under the blanket, and let his voice fill with disappointment.

"You ought to trust people more," he remarked.

She took a moment to answer. "My, you are sharp-eyed, aren't you?" she said waspishly.

"That's what you're paying me for," he reminded.

"It's just till I'm sure you don't have any wrong ideas," she said from under the blanket. "I've noticed the way you look at a woman."

"I understand," Fargo said. "That's why I've got my Colt right here beside me. I've noticed the way you've looked at me."

He saw her head lift. "Very funny," she sniffed. "I assure you you've nothing to worry about."

"That sure makes me feel better," he returned cheerfully. "My daddy warned me about headstrong females."

39

"Good night," she snapped crossly, and he knew she heard his soft chuckle. He turned on his side and closed his eyes, slept quickly as the night remained quiet.

3

Fargo woke with the morning sun as it crept down the mountainside, waking each tree and bush into all its brilliant fall color, as if an unseen hand set each afire. He lay quietly, listened, let his ears be his eyes. No sudden moves that might provoke unwelcome responses, perhaps the first lesson of living with wild creatures. He listened carefully but only the morning birdsongs reached his ears, and he separated their calls: chestnut-backed chickadees; field sparrows, always noisy; and the harsher cry of scrub jays. Most of the other birds had already flown south.

He heard the rustle of a blanket, rose onto one elbow to see Jennifer sitting up, rubbing sleep from her eyes, the deep-green nightdress and carrot-top hair making her look not unlike a tansy suddenly come upon in a meadow. A voluptuous tansy, he corrected.

" 'Morning," he called as he took a towel from his saddlebag and walked to the stream. He started to pull off shorts.

"What are you doing?" Jennifer's voice interrupted.

"Going to wake up and clean up in this cold, pure water," Fargo said.

"Right here?" She frowned.

"Why not? No need to go any farther," he said. "Come on and join me."

He saw her glare, flip angrily on her side, her back to him. "Kindly tell me when you've finished," she sniffed.

He laughed as he shed the shorts and stepped into the brook. The water, not yet warmed by the sun, sent an icy, tingling quiver through him. He immersed himself, not staying too long, and when he got out, he dried himself vigorously with the towel, rubbing warmth back into his body.

"Sure wakes you up. All yours now, honey," he called out as he bent to his clothes and began to dress.

Jennifer stood up, took a towel and clothes in her arms, shot him a disapproving glance, and started for the stream. She halted at the edge, felt his eyes on her.

"Will you go away till I've finished," she said, not really a question.

"Now, why would I do that?" he asked.

"Because that's what a gentleman would do," she snapped.

He smiled affably. "Being a gentleman wasn't part of the bargain," he said. He sat down, smiled again at her, and leaned back against a tree. Her lavender eyes blazed at him as she spun and strode away, walking up the bank of the stream until she was out of sight. His wild-creature hearing listened to the flow of the water as it changed when she stepped into it. He listened a few minutes longer, then rose and went to her blanket. The little pistol lay there and he picked it up. French-made, he saw, rimfire, five shots, black barrel and butt with a cross grain cut into it for easier gripping. He put it back on the blanket as he heard her returning. She had on the lime blouse, and for the first time he saw tiny points pushing against the material. The wonders of icy water . . . He smiled to himself and watched her saddle the dark-brown mare.

"We'll move, pick up something to eat along the way," he said.

"Fine with me," she said, and he waited till she mounted to start up the slope alongside the line of

42

maples. He found a stand of wild plums and halted for breakfast, continued on as the trail grew steeper again.

Jennifer trailed the packhorse behind her and he glanced back as the path rose more sharply once again. He let the pinto negotiate the steep incline his own way. When he reached the top, the steepness fell off and he dismounted and started back down on foot. Jennifer's mare was having trouble, the packhorse more.

"Get off her," he barked at Jennifer. "Let her go on her own." He continued down past the mare to where the packhorse was losing footing; he swung around behind the horse and put both hands on her rump. It added enough support to help the horse hold its footing, pull itself forward. Ahead, without Jennifer's weight in the saddle, the mare made the climb with only a little more sliding.

When he reached the top behind the packhorse, he halted, examined the two horses, and was satisfied they hadn't pulled any muscles. "Let them rest a few minutes," he said, his eyes hard as they focused on Jennifer. "Next time don't wait for me to tell you," he growled. "Up here your horse comes first, you second. Your horse is having trouble, use your damn head."

He saw her lips tighten, but she accepted the rebuke in silence. He rested another five minutes and then moved on again, the mountainside one unending upward climb, but the slopes were less steep for a while. When he halted to rest again, Jennifer's glance went to the sun.

"God, the day's on its way out and it seems we've hardly made any distance," she said frowning.

"It'll all be that way, slow going. One mile up here to every five miles in low country," Fargo told her, and he watched her pace back and forth impatiently. Her full-thighed legs moved in a graceful stride and the restlessness gave an added fire to her loveliness. She halted abruptly when she became aware of his eyes on her.

"Let's move," she said, swinging onto the dark-brown mare.

He climbed onto the Ovaro and set out again, grateful for trails that stayed at a slow incline. The sun had begun to track down the late-afternoon sky when he came to the cut that ran east-west across the mountain. Wide, with good timber cover, it would make for easy riding, and he started across it.

"This'll take us away from the maples," Jennifer protested.

"Not that far away," Fargo answered. "It'll be longer but easier on the horses." He ignored the disapproval in her eyes, started across the cut, and he saw it veered slowly to the left, back toward the maples. They had ridden perhaps another half-hour into the cut, he estimated, when he heard the flurry of shots from up ahead, not too far ahead. He frowned. He halted, exchanging frowns with Jennifer. Three more shots resounded, echoing against the sides of the cut. Mostly six-gun, with some heavier rifle fire mixed in, Fargo listened. He motioned Jennifer forward despite the apprehension in her face. Another flurry of shots resounded as they drew closer, and Fargo swung to the ground, led the Ovaro foward on foot. He halted after another dozen yards when three more shots resounded.

Jennifer came up to him leading her horse as he dropped the Ovaro's reins over a low branch. She did the same and stayed close to him. He crept forward, halted, dropped to one knee as the cut suddenly fell sharply away to become a small valley at the bottom of three heavily timbered slopes and one rock wall. Three wagons were clustered together at the bottom of the small valley, two high-sided Studebaker farm wagons fitted out with canvas covers and one Owensboro dray with canvas-covered stake sides.

He glimpsed figures by the wagons, hidden behind canvas and the sides of the wagons, and he lifted his gaze to peer across the high ground where he crouched. He spotted the figures, mostly obscured by the trees. He counted six men forming a loose half-circle that looked down on the wagons below, thought he glimpsed more, but he couldn't be certain. One thing was plain. They were holding the wagons trapped.

Fargo whispered to Jennifer as she knelt at his side. "Stay here and keep that hair of yours out of sight," he said.

"What are you going to do?" she returned.

"Get a closer look," he said, rose, and moved in a low crouch, circled to the left until he was opposite one end of the wagons. Staying hidden in the brush and the low mountain bushes, he moved down closer to the wagons below, halted halfway down the slope. He saw a woman with a baby in her arms huddled at the open tailgate of the nearest wagon. Two boys, not more than twelve each, lay under the wagon clutching old single-shot rifles they had to rest on wood boxes to fire. He peered along the wagons, saw a man hunched up beside the front wheel of the second Studebaker, a rifle in his hand. He made out two more shapes under the second wagon, and then he slowly pushed his way back up the slope to the top. He circled back to where Jennifer waited as dusk began to drift over the mountain.

"Well?" she asked sharply.

"Saw a woman with a baby, two young kids, a man, some others I couldn't make out," Fargo said. He was about to comment further when the voice interrupted, calling out from the center of the high ground, a voice that rolled down the slope with sonorous, prophetic overtones.

"Repent!" it said, and Fargo saw the outline of the figure rise in the center of the half-circle of men, the man little more than a dim bulk in the fast-lowering night. "Repent," the figure called out again. "You have until morning or you will rot in hell with the devil." The figure receded back into the trees and vanished from sight.

Fargo felt Jennifer pull at his arm. "Let's get out of here," she said.

"I told you, there's a woman and a baby trapped down there," Fargo said.

"We don't have time to play Good Samaritan," Jennifer returned tartly.

"You're all heart, aren't you, honey?" Fargo said. "I'm not much for playing good Samaritan, but I'm not for turning away from a woman trapped with a baby, either."

"You said yourself time was running out for finding Slattery," Jennifer persisted.

"It might be running out sooner for that woman down there," Fargo said. "We stay here till I can go down there and find out what this is all about. Something damn strange about it, I can feel that now."

"And then?" she pressed.

He shrugged. "Depends what I find out."

"No," Jennifer snapped. "Whatever you find out, we're leaving."

He didn't answer as he settled down to let the night grow deep. The stillness came to envelope the mountain cut and the little valley below, but he could hear the sounds of movement along the high ground and an occasional muttered word. The men forming the semicircle were settling down for the night. He could feel Jennifer's angriness coming at him in silent waves through the darkness, and he stayed motionless till the moon rose over the trees. The land had grown quiet when he moved to a crouch.

"I won't stand for this, Fargo," Jennifer hissed.

"Sit down, then," Fargo answered as he disappeared down the mountainside. He moved in a sideways crawl, clinging to the mountain brush and circling to come out at the far end of the wagons below. He continued to descend till he reached the level ground, not a half-dozen yards from the first of the canvas-topped Studebakers. He dropped low, spied the form under a blanket beside the rear wheels of the wagon. He peered along the line of the other wagons, glimpsed two more sleeping figures wrapped in blankets under the second wagon, and he crept forward to the nearest wagon, edged closer, halted as the figure turned. A girl, he saw, straight black hair. She turned again in a restless half-sleep, and he saw an attractive face, good, strong planes, a straight nose, a strong face. Fargo reached out, pressed one big hand over the girl's mouth.

Her eyes snapped awake at once as fear seized her face. "Easy," Fargo whispered. "Easy." She stared at him from above his hand. "I'm not one of them," he said reassuringly. She continued to stare at him. "I was passing through. Maybe I can help you. I don't know," he said, keeping his voice calm, and he thought he saw her eyes turn a fraction less frightened. "My name's Fargo . . . Skye Fargo," he said, and took his hand from her mouth.

She started to push herself to a sitting position and he waited, let her sit up, and saw a slender figure, long-waisted, with a graceful neck and modest breasts that pressed into a brown shirt with surprisingly prominent little points. He couldn't make out the color of her eyes in the moonlight, but there was more strength than fear in them now. "What's all this about? Why are you being pinned down here?" he asked.

"It's the preacher and some of his followers," the girl said.

"The preacher?" Fargo frowned.

The girl nodded, her face grave. "Preacher Roan, head of the Church of the Apostles," she said.

"That doesn't tell me why he has you pinned down here," Fargo said.

"We were part of his followers," she said. "Until we found out he was a crazy man. We decided to leave. We didn't want any more of him or his church. He beats people, kills them in the name of the Lord. He's a crazy man and we wanted out."

"But Preacher Roan had other ideas," Fargo remarked.

She nodded again. "Nobody leaves the Church of the Apostles, he told us. Nobody. We'd be turning our backs on the Lord and we'd have to die for that. We thought it was just more of his crazy preaching, and we packed up and left. But he came after us, attacked our wagons. We tried to get away from him into the mountains and got ourselves trapped in this cut."

"How many are you?" Fargo asked. "I saw a woman with a baby?"

"That's be Annie Stewart. Her husband was killed in the preacher's first attack, along with four of our men. There are only a few of us left: Annie and the baby, the two Dillworth boys and their mother, Ben O'Toole and his wife, Seth and Mary Brown, and me. I'm Clare Todd," she said, and paused as her eyes lingered on the chiseled handsomeness of the big man in front of her.

Fargo's glance left her as he saw the movement to his right, a man emerging from under the next wagon, start toward them with rifle in hand.

"Clare, who's that with you?" the man called.

"It's all right, Seth. Come over here," Clare Todd called.

The man approached, middle-aged, a short beard, his face mirroring surprise and uncertainty.

"This man's come to maybe help us," Clare said.

The man halted, his eyes peering at Fargo. "Where'd you come from, mister?" he asked.

"Up there." Fargo gestured. "Came onto the firing and decided to find out what it was all about."

"I told him, Seth," the girl said, and Fargo saw

her eyes on him, appraising, studying. She had real beauty in her high-planed face, he decided, beauty and a kind of quiet strength.

Seth Brown regarded Fargo with weariness and dejection. "How are you going to help us?" he asked. "There are eight or more up there."

Fargo half-shrugged. "Start by talking to this Preacher Roan. Maybe I can convince him to back off," he said.

Seth Brown grunted derisively. "Never, not that crazy man. He's out to kill us all for turning away from him."

Clare cut in quickly. "It's worth a try, Seth. We've nothing to lose by the man trying," she said.

"You do what you've been doing, stay under cover till I get back to you," Fargo said.

"When will you do that?" she asked.

"Tomorrow night for sure. Maybe a lot sooner," Fargo said.

Seth Brown nodded agreement and Clare Todd rose to stand beside Fargo. Her slenderness stayed, he noted, narrow hips that curved into long legs under a black riding skirt. The high-planed face held more than strength, a lean wildness in it, he took note as she walked to the end of the wagon with him.

"Why are you doing this?" she asked.

"Started by all this being in my way. Now, if what you say is right, I figure you're owed a chance. We've enough crazies in the world."

"I'm right," Clare Todd said with a flat grimness in her voice. "I hope you can do it. I'll be beholden to you."

"I'll keep that in mind." He smiled as he began to climb the slope, retrace steps up the sides of the cut. He saw her watch him till he was out of sight, and he continued on to the top of the steep sides. The pale moonlight outlined Jennifer as he returned and sank down beside her.

49

"Well?" she snapped out at once, the lone word dripping with ice. There was no melting of it when he finished telling her what he'd learned. "We're not getting involved in this," she said.

"You telling me you don't care about a woman and a baby? You don't care if those people are killed by some crazy?" Fargo asked.

He saw her eyes flicker but her face stayed set. "I'll be sorry, but I'm not taking care of the world," she said. "And neither are you, not on my time."

"I'll throw in three extra days, how's that?" he snapped with acid.

"Unsatisfactory," she tossed back.

His voice grew hard. "Tough shit, honey. Maybe I can save those people. Maybe not. But I'm going to give it a try."

She spun away, sat down against a tree, and he could feel her simmering. He walked back to where he'd left the horses, took out his bedroll, undressed, and lay down. Jennifer came along soon after, undressed in the trees, and simmered under her blanket. Fargo ignored the waves of anger that emanated from her, and he found himself thinking about Clare Todd. He sensed something different about the girl, something unusual in that high-planed face, her figure more than simply slender, a lean strength to it. Her eyes had held more than questions, a curiosity that went beyond the moment at hand. He half-smiled as he closed his eyes and let sleep come. The morning would bring another kind of answer. He slept soundly, came awake twice at sounds only to find they were Jennifer's restless stirring.

Morning came in on a crisp wind and he grimaced as he felt the chill against his face, grateful to see a bright, clear sky. The only dark cloud was Jennifer's glower as, finished dressing, she returned to where he adjusted the cinch around the Ovaro's belly. "I don't suppose I can expect a hand from you in this," he remarked.

"You suppose right," Jennifer snapped.

"Then stay here, be quiet, and keep out of sight," Fargo said.

"And twiddle my thumbs while I'm waiting around," Jennifer returned hotly. "Dammit, Fargo, this isn't fair. You hired on for me. I'm paying you."

"You're paying me, not buying me, honey," Fargo said. She tossed him an angry glance as he mounted the Ovaro and rode away. He moved forward along the edge of the steep slope, had ridden some fifty yards when he saw the figures emerge from the tree cover, three men with rifles, then two more. A sixth figure came into view, and Fargo saw the others make way for him as he came forward. Fargo kept the Ovaro walking slowly, saw the man halt in his path, tall, clothed in a black preacher's coat and black hat, a narrow, sallow face with a small, pointed beard at the end of a long chin. But it was his eyes that held Fargo's gaze, pale-blue yet burning with an inner intensity, as though glass were somehow able to catch fire. Fargo glanced at the others who had now all stepped into view. Seth Brown had been right. Eight, he counted silently, each face grave, severe, each pair of eyes a paler version of the preacher's burning gaze.

"I am Preacher Roan," the man intoned, his voice strong. "Who art thou?"

"Fargo," the big man said. "Some call me the Trailsman."

"What do you want here?" the preacher asked, the tone commanding.

"I was passing through and wondered why you're shooting at those folks down there," Fargo said casually.

"Why do you care?" the man asked.

Fargo shrugged. "Saw a woman with a baby down there," he said.

"She and the child are no better than the others. They are all possessed of the devil," the preacher said, letting his tones ring out prophetically. "They

51

will not repent their evil ways and so the Lord will smite them down."

Fargo kept his tone bland. "How's He going to do that?" he asked.

"He will smite them through me. I am His servant. I do His bidding," the man replied.

"And He told you to do this," Fargo said calmly, almost casually.

The preacher nodded, and the burning in the pale-blue eyes seemed to grow more intense. "His voice has come to me many times. Those whose souls the devil has entered must be destroyed. Even the repentant must be punished," the man said. "I have given them their chance to repent. They refuse it."

"Maybe I could talk to them," Fargo said.

The preacher frowned. "If they will not repent for me, they certainly will not repent for you," he said with righteous indignance.

"I don't know anything about this repenting stuff," Fargo said. "I'd just hate to see all those folks killed. Maybe I could convince them they haven't got a chance. They don't know how many men you've got up here. I'd just lay it to them the way it is. Maybe they'd listen to a stranger with no ax to grind."

Fargo waited, kept his face mildly interested, and saw the preacher frown as thoughts turned behind the burning pale-blue eyes.

"Perhaps you are right," the man said, turning the burning eyes on him. "Perhaps they would listen to you. Go down, tell them what you've seen. They must put down their weapons, come out, and fall to their knees and repent."

"What happens then?" Fargo asked casually.

The burning eyes were unable to conceal the edge of craftiness that came into them. "The Lord will speak to me. He will proclaim His will to me," the preacher said.

"Sounds fair enough," Fargo drawled. "I'll just ride on down and give it a try."

The preacher gestured with a sweeping motion of his arm, and Fargo sent the Ovaro over the top of the high land, down the gentler slope in the center. He let the horse negotiate his downward climb, let Preacher Roan's words hang in his mind. He grunted harshly to himself. The preacher was a dyed-in-the-wool crazy, all right, but he'd been quick to see his chance. He'd kill two birds with one stone, massacre the kneeling penitents and proclaim the Lord's punishment all in a single instant.

Fargo spied Clare Todd standing beside the big Owensboro as he reached the wagons and dismounted. The others came up, Seth Brown in the lead, the two young boys behind him, a sad-eyed woman beside them. He waited, let the rest gather, and fastened his gaze on Clare Todd. Dark-blue eyes, he noted in passing.

"You were right on both counts," Fargo said. "He's a crazy and he won't back off. He wants you to lay down your guns, come out, and fall to your knees and repent."

"And he'll shoot us all," Seth Brown said.

"I figure that, too," Fargo agreed. "But if you don't, he'll come down and wipe you out the hard way."

"We are trapped," the woman said.

"Maybe not," Fargo answered, saw the questions in Clare's steady gaze. "I'm going back up, tell him that I couldn't convince you to repent, and go on my way. Only I won't go far." His eyes fastened on the two young boys. "You two are the smallest. Stay behind on the far side of each horse and start leading the wagons. Hold them by the cheek strap and move them forward. From up there, it'll look as if you're all starting to try to move out. They'll have to come into the open to get down the slope. When they're halfway down, you start shooting and I'll blast them from the side. We'll catch them in a two-way fire."

53

Fargo watched the small group exchange glances. "It might just work," Seth said. Fargo half-turned the Ovaro, met Clare Todd's unwavering eyes. She nodded and half-shrugged.

"Start the wagons rolling ten minutes from when I reach the top," Fargo said, and spurred the Ovaro forward up the slope. He let the pinto take the climb unhurriedly and a grim smile touched his lips. He couldn't see her, but he wagered Jennifer had crept closer, watched from behind the thick brush somewhere. It all meant too much to her to allow her to stay back and simply wait, he grunted silently.

Preacher Roan came forward when Fargo reached the top of the slope, his burning gaze questioning.

Fargo let himself seem chagrined. "You were right, Preacher. Couldn't get them to listen to reason," he said.

Preacher Roan seemed more pleased than disappointed, and his face took on righteous vindication. "They refuse to repent," he thundered. "They have defied the Lord and the Church of the Apostles. I must smite them down. His arm shall be my arm. His sword shall be my sword."

"And you're going to enjoy your smiting, aren't you?" Fargo remarked.

The burning eyes bored into him. "To do the Lord's work is a joyful task," the man intoned.

"One more thing to remember," Fargo said. "I'll be riding on now." He moved the Ovaro forward unhurriedly, through the line of the preacher's followers. He'd reached the edge of the far side of the slope when the preacher's voice called after him. "Stay and be one of us, Fargo," the man said.

Fargo halted, looked back. "No, thanks. Got my own ways to go," he said.

"Are you of the Lord or of the devil, Fargo?" the preacher called.

"I'm still shopping around," Fargo said, and spurred the Ovaro into the trees and out of sight. He rode another half-dozen yards, turned, slid from the horse, and returned to the edge of the trees. He pulled the big Sharps rifle from its saddle holster, knelt on one knee, had just lain the gun across his leg when he heard the preacher's roar.

"They move. They try to flee," the man shouted. "Destroy them. Follow me. Descend on them with the wrath of the Lord in your weapons."

The Trailsman watched the preacher start down the slope on horseback, his followers going with him. Fargo felt the frown dig into his brow as he saw the riders start their descent. Ten, he muttered under his breath. Not eight. Ten. Two had stayed back in the trees out of sight. He watched the line of trees behind the edge of the slope, but no others appeared and he returned his gaze to the preacher. The man was pushing his horse, in the clear now, almost halfway down the slope.

Fargo raised the big Sharps, his finger on the trigger, and held his fire a moment longer until the rest of the preacher's men were in the clear. His finger tightened on the trigger and the rifle's deep, heavy bark resounded. The horseman nearest him seemed to leap in the saddle before he toppled to the ground.

Fargo swung the Sharps, fired off two more rounds, and two more of the preacher's men fell. He heard the volley of shots explode from the wagons below and saw two of the horsemen topple from their mounts. He fired again, as fast as he could, as another volley resounded from below.

The preacher's men tried to wheel their horses on the slope as the cross fire poured into them, and three more went down. There were only three left, desperately trying to turn their mounts, and Fargo saw the preacher leap from his horse, roll into the brush that dotted the slope, half-crawl, half-leap forward behind the brush. He let the fire from below finish off the other two as he watched the figure in the brush pulling itself up toward him. The man had found a row of mountain shrub that gave him cover and only the top of his black hat flashed into view. He pulled himself upward toward the edge of the slope, neared it when Fargo rose, the rifle aimed.

"That's close enough, Preacher," he said.

The black hat halted, stayed motionless, and finally rose as the preacher stood up, clambered to the top of the slope. He took another step closer. "Would thou shoot a man of God?" he asked.

The rifle stayed trained on his figure. "Wouldn't like to," Fargo answered, "but I could force myself."

Preacher Roan took another step toward him, reached inside his black preacher's coat with one hand.

Fargo's finger tightened on the trigger. "Easy, now," he growled.

The man drew his hand out and with it a black, leather-covered Bible with a gold cross stamped into it. "The Good Book says you can be forgiven your sins, Fargo," the man intoned.

"Good. Now, you just stay right there, Preacher," Fargo growled.

The man opened the Bible, held the book up in front of him. "Here, I shall read you the words, Matthew twelve," he began.

"Some other time," Fargo interrupted. He saw the preacher lower the Bible, and his eyes widened in surprise as the round end of the short-barreled revolver appeared over the top of the book. "Damn," he swore, and he dived to one side as the shot exploded. He felt the bullet graze the tip of his boot as he hit the ground and rolled. Another shot plowed into a bush inches from his head. He rolled again, dropped rifle, and a third shot tore back from a tree just behind him; then he had the big Colt out, fired from the ground as the preacher raced at him, the black coat flying out behind him, the revolver in his hand.

Fargo's first shot caught the man in the shoulder, the second one tore into his chest. The preacher half-turned, twisted, tottered sideways, the black coat flapping wildly. He looked not unlike a giant wounded black crow as he fell, arms outspread, jerking in spasms until he lay still.

Fargo pulled himself to his feet, walked over to the Bible beside the figure, saw the hollowed-out pages where the gun had been concealed. He nudged the book with the toe of his boot. "Says something in there about he that lies won't escape," he muttered at the still figure. He turned away, walked to the Ovaro, put the Sharps into the saddle holster, and swung onto the horse. As he started down to the wagons below, his eyes peered across the edge of the slope, caught the flash of orange-red hair, then Jennifer's figure as she stepped from the trees. He waved a hand at her as he continued down.

Seth Brown was the first to greet him when he reached the wagons. "It worked, by God. It worked," the man enthused. "We'll be forever in your debt, Fargo."

"Forget it. Go your way, find your happiness. I'm glad I came by at the right time," Fargo told the others as they gathered. Their murmurs of appreciation finally died away as the little group turned to their wagons. All except the slender figure with the black hair that stayed leaning against the tailgate of the Owensboro, dark-blue eyes narrowed on him.

"Where are you going now?" Clare Todd asked.

"Into the mountains," Fargo said. "Been hired to take someone."

Her thin eyebrows arched. "At this time?" she commented.

"Maybe we'll get lucky." He shrugged.

"Got room for one more?" Clare Todd asked, and it was his turn to arch brows. "I'm at loose ends.

There's nothing to keep me on with the others. And I could help you."

"How?"

"I was born in the Medicine Bow Range, lived up there till I was ten. I know things about these mountains most folks don't know," she said, and his eyes questioned further. "My father was a miner. He tried to work the mountains. Not much luck, but he took an Arapaho wife, my mother," she went on. "When she died, he sent me to live with his people in Boulder."

Fargo turned the offer in his mind, her eyes adding to the appeal of it. "It won't be a picnic," he said. "Could be nobody will come back."

She shrugged. "Never had much to come back to," she said.

"You're young for that kind of talk," Fargo said.

Her little smile held wryness. "When you don't fit anywhere, when you're always an outsider, the world doesn't hold a whole lot for you."

He let his lips purse in thought as her eyes stayed on him. He saw her glance away, up to the top of the slope where Jennifer's orange-red hair gleamed, an eye-catching burst of color.

"She the one hired you?" Clare asked, and Fargo nodded and saw the tiny smile play with her lips. "Figures," she said.

"Why?" he asked.

"Money wouldn't be enough to send a man like you on a fool's chase," Clare answered.

"It's strictly business," Fargo said.

"Think it'll stay that way?" Clare half-laughed, the lean planes in her face suddenly softening.

"Likely," he said.

"Then I can do more than help you," she said.

He let his own laugh echo hers. "Why not? Get your gear," he said. His glance went to the top of the slope as Clare hurried to the Owensboro. His lips pulled into a tight smile. Jennifer would be less than agreeable. She wouldn't want anyone else along, much less another female. He didn't spend thought on the reasons now. They'd come clear when the time came to close the gaps in her story. He swung onto the Ovaro and let the horse pull itself to where Jennifer waited, her face still angry.

"Can we move on now?" she snapped.

"We'll be having company," he said.

"That girl you were talking to down there?" Jennifer glared, and he nodded. "Forget it," she snapped.

"She's half-Arapaho, grew up here in the Medicine Bow Range. I figure she'll be of real help," Fargo said.

"You figure she'll be real nice in your bedroll," Jennifer accused.

He let himself look injured. "You've got me all wrong," he said.

"Hah!" she snorted.

"Now, I won't say I'd object to that, but it's not the reason I'm taking her along," Fargo said.

"Well, I object. You're here to ride trail, not tail," Jennifer spit back. "I'm paying you and I expect one hundred percent of your time and your thoughts. I won't have you mooning about over some little piece of baggage."

"You making me a better offer?" He grinned and saw her lips thin.

"Certainly not," she said indignantly.

He shrugged. "She comes along. If she can cut time in finding Slattery, you'll be glad for it," he said. He turned from her, watched Clare near on a gray gelding, a short-legged horse good for mountain work; she had a pack strapped on behind her saddle. Clare reached the top and Fargo saw her meet Jennifer's angry eyes with unruffled calm. He made introductions and Jennifer's face stayed as if made of ice.

"You don't favor my coming along," Clare remarked.

"The understatement of the century," Jennifer

59

snapped. She spun on her heel and stalked back to where her horse waited.

Fargo turned, started to lead the way along the top of the slope, stayed on the high ground until the slow circle returned to the line of maples again. He began the slow climb upward paralleling the scarlet-leafed trees, Jennifer behind him, Clare drawing up in the rear behind Jennifer's packhorse. He watched Clare's eyes on the packhorse as the animal had trouble getting over a sudden rise of rock and brush, and when Fargo called a rest soon after, she knelt down beside him.

"You're following the maples. Why?" she asked.

"Got a sort-of map that tells us to," he answered. "Man named Slattery drew it, supposed to be following it."

"Climbing alongside them like this is the hard way," she said. "There used to be elk and deer trails inside the maples. I'd guess they're still there."

"They go up the mountains?" Fargo asked.

"They cross back and forth while doing it." She nodded. "They'd be a lot easier on the horses if you can find them."

He got to his feet. "I'll find them," he said, and climbed onto the Ovaro. He turned the horse into the thick forest of the brilliantly colored trees, moved slowly, his eyes sweeping back and forth unceasingly. They'd gone almost an hour into the maples when he halted, motioned to where three trees were stripped bare of bark at the lower portion of the trunk. He turned, followed the line of the trees, soon found others stripped away, and then the path came into view, wide enough for two horses to move abreast, the ground worn smooth, an easy-riding trail.

The path led upward at an angle, crossed another that climbed farther, and he followed the second trail up. He saw the shadows beginning to lengthen, the thick timberland quick to embrace darkness, and he found a glen where a bower of maples formed a shield against the night wind that had already started to blow. He called a halt and the dark swept down on the glen before the horses were unsaddled. Fargo took some beef jerky from one of the packs and they ate in silence and weariness.

Finished, Clare took her pack and unrolled a blanket, placed it against one side of the trees. "This will be my first real sleep in three nights," she said.

"Do make the most of it," Jennifer remarked as she went into the trees to undress.

Clare came over to Fargo, her eyes coolly amused. "She'd like you to herself," the girl said.

"No, she's just being bitchy," Fargo said.

"That's only part of it," Clare said. "Are you disappointed about my being so tired?"

"There'll be a lot of nights," Fargo said.

"Starting with tomorrow," Clare said, turned, and went to her blanket, managed to shed clothes under the blanket as Jennifer returned and placed her blanket on the other side of the trees. Fargo settled into his bedroll and watched the two young women adjust themselves under their blankets. A wry smile touched his lips. Contrasts in loveliness, he mused: Clare's promise veiled in dark-blue orbs, Jennifer unveiled angry disapproval; Clare understated strength, Jennifer headstrong fire. Oil and water? A combination that couldn't mix? He went to sleep on the question, certain only that the answer would come soon enough.

He slept quickly, and the morning arrived unexpectedly warm as he rose, watched Jennifer sit up in the green nightdress, stretch, her full breasts pulling the material smooth against her. Clare emerged from under her blanket in a loose, oversize man's shirt that reached down midway on her thigh and made her look not unlike a little girl.

"Indian summer," Jennifer observed as the sun beamed warmth.

Fargo grunted. He'd always had mixed feelings about Indian summer, uncertain whether it was Mother Nature's benevolent side, giving her creatures a reprieve, a last chance to prepare, or nature toying with her creatures, lulling them into false security.

Clare's voice broke into his thoughts. "There's a mountain spring up near here. Sits in the sun," she said.

"Let's go," Fargo said, and began to pull on clothes.

Clare led the way, took only one wrong turn before she found the spring, a pool almost perfectly round in shape fed by an underground mountain spring that bubbled fountainlike in the center. Clare took her blanket and Jennifer came up with a large bath towel.

"You two first. I'll stand watch," Fargo said.

Jennifer's glance was sharp. "I'm quite sure what you'll watch," she said. He didn't reply. "I suppose it's too much to expect you to be a gentleman," she said.

"Yep," he said cheerfully.

She hissed a reply under her breath as she spun away.

Fargo scanned the surroundings, found a flat rock that looked down on the little pool while affording a good view of the area. He climbed to the top of the rock, scanned the circle of trees. Nothing moved except the swoop of birds, unbothered, in normal flight, and he lowered his gaze to the sunlit pool that bubbled in its center. Jennifer shed clothes behind a bush and emerged wrapped in the large towel, walked to the water with it, and let it fall away as she slid into the pool. He caught a glimpse of nothing but her back, smooth, well-modeled shoulder blades.

Clare halted at the water's edge, pulled the outsize man's shirt from herself, and stretched in the sun, a lean, slender body, completely tanned, a body of angels and planes more than curves. Modest breasts lay tight against her slender rib cage, a little flat with large, brown-pink nipples and dark, large circles behind each point. She moved gracefully, almost catlike, flat buttocks and slender legs that held an understated shapeliness. She half-turned toward him, and he saw a flat abdomen and a small, dark triangle. She slipped into the water the way an otter moves, pushing off onto her back, turning lazily, a flash of breasts and glistening points breaking the surface of the water.

Jennifer bathed and dived under the water, only the carrot-topped face and shoulders surfacing. Finished, she swam to the shore, reached out and took the big towel, held it up to block his view, and stepped from the pool behind it, wrapping it around her in one quick motion. Clare walked from the water, her tan body glistening, shoulders thrown back, slender legs taking long steps; she took up her towel and dried herself vigorously. Jennifer's remark drifted up to where he sat and he saw Clare pause.

"You've obviously never heard of modesty," Jennifer snapped.

"You've never heard of being natural," Clare returned.

Jennifer turned, stalked into the trees, and Clare pulled the outsize shirt over herself.

Fargo's glance swept the high land again and he climbed back down to the pool, satisfied they were alone.

"You can finish dressing and saddle up," he told Clare as Jennifer came from the trees in a dark-green blouse and black riding skirt. She hurried away as he began to pull off clothes and Clare followed her, tossing a quick glance back, he noted, as he stepped into the pool. He bathed quickly, hurried out, stood in the warmth of the sun, and felt it dry his skin as he stretched. A gust of wind, surprisingly warm, came to help the sun finish the job, and he was able to dress in minutes.

He returned to the glen to find both Jennifer and Clare in the saddle, waiting, each cloaked in her own silence. He swung onto the Ovaro, started to move through the maples and noted that Clare brought up in the rear again. The deer and elk trails began to disappear, trailing away into timberland. He saw the pieces of fur against the trees as he rode upward. The animals filtered through the higher mountain country in small groups, forming trails only lower down, it seemed, and he led the way out of the maples to climb upward alongside once more. By midafternoon the warm wind had changed character, taking on a sharpness, and he saw Jennifer don the tan buckskin jacket. He halted at a long log where one side sprouted a line of blood-red mushrooms. "Russulas," he said as he dismounted, felt the mushrooms with his fingers, pressing one after the other atop the decaying log.

The grimness was in the single word he muttered. "Dry," he said, his lips tight. "Sign of cold weather near."

"Not up here," Clare said. "They're always dry up here. The cool nights, maybe, or the air itself. I never knew how soft they were until I left the mountains."

Fargo nodded, grateful for the reassurance in her words. He mounted and led the way on, slowed when the ascent suddenly steepened, felt the Ovaro digging hooves deep into the soil to make the sudden sharp climb. He halted the horse, let the animal back down to where Jennifer had halted. "That packhorse will never make it. I'm not sure my Ovaro can do it," he said. "We'll have to detour, find a better spot."

"We keep going away from the maples. The map says stay alongside them," Jennifer protested.

"We'll come back to them. I'll bet Slattery had to

detour plenty, too," Fargo answered, and moved off across the side of the mountain. He rode slowly, glanced back frequently, and finally spotted an upward passage a little less punishing. He took it, reached the top after a half-hour of hard climbing, and halted as the land leveled out for a dozen yards. He was dismounted as Jennifer reached him, his eyes on the packhorse. "We've got to lighten his load. He's limping now," Fargo said, gesturing to the packhorse.

Jennifer dismounted, frowning. "I didn't notice him limping," she said.

"I did. That's all that counts," Fargo said gruffly. "What've you got loaded on that horse?"

"Tins of food," Jennifer said as Clare dismounted, began to untie the packs.

"What kind of food?" Fargo questioned.

"Some tinned beef. Biscuits, hardtack, beef jerky, some tins of lard, things I thought would come in handy," Jennifer replied.

"What else?" Fargo pressed, eyeing the sizable packs on the horse.

"Extra canvas, extra clothes, a big tarpaulin," Jennifer said, paused, and saw Fargo waiting, his eyes hard. "Two shovels, a pick, an iron strongbox," she said, half-shrugged defensively. "In case Slattery had buried the money," she said.

"And the strongbox to carry it back," he finished, and she nodded.

He turned to the packhorse and helped Clare untie the rope. "Everything goes except the hardtack, the beef jerky, two tins of the beef and two of the biscuits, and the tarpaulin," he said.

"Just a second. That's not right," Jennifer protested. "I packed those things because I need them."

"You just changed your mind about needing them," Fargo said. "This horse can't carry more than that. He hasn't the legs for this mountain work. I told you that."

"I'll carry my extra clothes," Jennifer said.

"Suit yourself," Fargo said, undid the last of the packs, and spilled the contents on the ground. He had the horse repacked to carry a fraction of the load as the shadows began to lengthen. He saw Jennifer start to collect the shovels and pick and carry them to her horse. "Leave it," he growled.

"I'm not asking anyone to carry them," she said.

"You're asking the horse. Leave it," Fargo said.

She let the tools slide to the ground, glared at him.

He ignored her, swung onto the pinto, and started forward again. The mountain took mercy on them and let the incline stay negotiable, and Fargo quickened the pace, moved through the deepening shadows until he reined up suddenly, his eyes holding at a little half-circle to one side of their path. He dismounted, knelt on one knee as he examined the ground.

"What is it?" Jennifer asked.

"Somebody camped here for a night," Fargo said. "Couple of weeks ago. One man, two horses."

"Slattery," Jennifer said, excitement catching her voice.

"Likely," Fargo surmised as he remounted and continued on. He found a place to make camp as the night turned the mountain into blackness. He made a small fire, just large enough to warm the beef jerky and to let each of them have a cup of coffee brewed with water from their canteens. He set his bedroll off to one side, partway into the trees, and lay quietly as Jennifer slid under her blanket, Clare rolling herself up in hers. He lay awake as the moon rose to flicker a pale light through the leaves and the wind blew with an added night edge. He had checked the land behind them as they climbed and was satisfied no one followed. But it was too early, he reminded himself. Anyone following could do so easily enough, their trail clear. He had more than enough to do to

66

try to pick up Slattery's movements without trying to hide his own trail. He continued to let his thoughts idle, glimpsed the moon through the trees, three-quarters full, started to turn on his side when he caught the faint sound, soft footsteps, barefoot steps. He rose onto one elbow, his hand automatically closing around the big Colt at his side when he saw the figure loom in the faint light, an odd shape wrapped in the blanket, faintly ominous.

"Fargo," Clare whispered as she sank down to her knees. He held the bedroll open and she unwrapped herself from the blanket, had the loose shirt on underneath, he saw as she slid into the bedroll beside him. "Were you waiting for me to come?" she asked.

"Wondering more than waiting," he said.

She smelled faintly musky, a sensuous odor, and he watched her pull the shirt off, sit up, the modest breasts lying almost against his chest. Her eyes searched his, an appraising stare. "It's not just to say thanks for what you did," she said.

"Good," he said. "Wanting's better than thanking."

Her voice dropped to a breathy whisper. "I want, Fargo, I want. From the first moment I saw you," Clare Todd said. "You're big and good-looking, but it's not just that. It's something else."

"Such as?" he asked.

"Something that touches inside me, tells me you'd understand me," she said, shrugged. "I feel things like that inside. I know, somehow, I just know."

His mouth found hers, parted her lips, and her tongue slid out at once, slow turnings inside his mouth, touching, drawing back and coming forward again. His tongue answered, pressed her back, and she welcomed him, her lips firm yet soft. His hands covered her breasts and the brown-pink nipples pressed firmly into his palms.

Clare turned her slender, angular body for him, lay on her back, and her hands caressed the nape of his

67

neck, gently pulled his face down until his lips found one of the modest, slightly flat breasts. He sucked it into his mouth and felt the little shudder go through her, sucked deeper and felt the tip come against the roof of his mouth. He caressed her breast with his lips, his tongue, tracing slow circles around the erect little tip. "Ah . . . aaaaah," Clare breathed as he did the same with the other breast, and he felt her pelvis moving, a slow, rubbing motion, and she began to move her thighs against each other, a sinuous rubbing, and tiny sounds came from somewhere inside her, little half-gasps.

His hand moved down her slender figure, a slow path across the prominent ribs, the almost concave little abdomen, wandered back and forth across her flat belly, and her legs rubbed together more rapidly, turned as one, falling to one side, then the other. His hand found the beginnings of the little black triangle, smaller than it had appeared from atop the rock, smaller and hardly any curl to it, a springy flatness that rested rather than pushed against his hand. But the little mound rose high and firm, and as his finger slipped over it to the mouth of the little triangle, Clare's legs fell open, not unlike the way the leaves fell from the fall trees. His fingers touched the soft lips, moist, quivering, and he heard the sound begin from inside her, half-moan, half-song, deep, low, rising and falling in rhythm with the undulating movement of her hips. Her hand clasped atop his, pressed his fingers into her. "Yes, yes, please, Fargo . . . please, rub me, hold me, oh, oh . . ." The words came whispered between the half-moan singsong sounds. He caressed the moist soft lips, gently rubbed the little center that quivered for him.

Clare's flat abdomen sucked in still further as she drew her pelvis in, thrust forward suddenly, seemed to try to swallow his hand, and he touched deeper into the warm, moist tunnel, stroked the top, slow, sensual strokings. "Ah . . . oh . . . uuuum . . . uuuummmmm. . . ." The half-moan, half-song grew stronger, and he watched Clare's slender form half-turn, half-twist, slow motions accompanied by the moaning song, a sinuous loveliness to her almost snakelike movements. The dark-blue eyes stared at him, veiled now, caught in a very personal world, feeling more than seeing. She half-turned again, lifted herself, and rubbed her breasts up and down his chest, and he felt her slip away from his hand, legs moving, trying to curl around his powerful frame. He raised himself to let her and felt the two slender shapes press around his hips, lift, lock around the lower part of his back. He let his pulsating, eager organ move into her, felt the warm wetness flow around him deliciously, and he moved deeper.

"Mmmmmm . . . mmmmmmmaaaaah . . . mmmmmmm," she breathed in the low half-song moan. Her body continued its sinuous twisting as her hips rose to draw him in farther. He felt the soft wall of her against his organ with unexpected quickness, and he drew back, thrust forward again, pressing against her. "Mmmmm . . . ah . . . aaaaah . . . uuuummmmm. . . ." The singsong moan continued and every part of her seemed to twist and turn as he moved steadily inside her—legs, arms, torso, modest breasts falling to one side, flipping to the other as she twisted. Her hands slid up and down his body—chest, arms, back, closed around the firmness of his buttocks—and suddenly the half-moan song took on another note, rising in pitch, a sudden urgency in it. He felt her legs begin to press hard against him and the sinuous motions of her body quickened. Her hands dug into his buttocks. "Fargo . . . Fargo . . . I'm coming . . . uuuummmm . . . I'm coming . . . uuuummmm . . . I'm coming," she cried out, and he felt her softness pressing hard against him as she began to explode. The half-moan became a muffled deep cry into his chest as she clung to him and her

69

rear slid along the bedroll as she slammed herself against his maleness, sliding herself back and forth in quick spasms of motion until she held against him, her legs stiffening around him.

"Ah . . . ah, God, aaaiiiii . . . aiiiiiiii . . . oh, yes," Clare cried against him. He held inside her, ramrod rigid as she quivered, clung to the wild moment of all-encompassing ecstasy. He waited, held with her, until he felt her begin to subside, and then he let himself explode inside her.

"Oh, my God," she screamed against him, threw her slender body back into a convex arch, every muscle tensed, her fists pounding against the ground, lips open gasping in air until the exploding came to a halt inside her. "Oh, no . . . no,"she protested even as she sank to the ground, totally spent, and he joined her in the sweet emptiness, desire drained into itself.

Slowly she pulled herself against him, moving with the same sinuousness as when she'd made love. She lay draped half over him as he lay on his back. One slender leg inserted itself between his powerful thighs and rested lightly against his crotch. She traced her fingers idly over his chest, and her dark-blue eyes looked at him with a kind of awesome gravity. "I knew it would be special with you. I knew it," she said. Her fingers traced a line up his right forearm, found the half-moon scar, and halted, their very touch questioning.

"A she-grizzly," Fargo said. "Surprised her and almost paid for it with my neck."

She looked away in thought, stared into the night. "You pay for mistakes," she said.

"You've more than that in mind," he said.

"I'm wondering what you'll pay for coming up here at this time," she said. "Why is she following this Slattery?"

He thought for a moment. She had come along. She deserved knowing. He told her how and why

Jennifer had come to hire him, told her Jennifer's story just as he'd been given it.

Clare peered at his face when he finished. "You don't take her story all the way," she commented.

He smiled as he frowned. "Now, what makes you think that?" he asked.

Her breasts rubbed against his chest as she shrugged. "No reasons I can tell, only you told it too carefully," she said, and Fargo felt the wryness come into his smile. Female intuition, he grunted silently. It never ceased to surprise him, that special instinct, the uncanny ability to pinpoint the unsaid.

"I've a few questions that still need answering," he admitted. "When the time comes."

"You think there's time to find this man Slattery?" Clare asked.

"If we get lucky," he answered, grinned at her. "Luck's doing right by me so far," he added, pressed one hand into her tight little rear, ran his fingers up onto the small of her back, up to her waist. He could almost close his hand half around the narrowness of her waist, he noted.

She smiled and he felt her leg begin to move slowly up and down between his thighs, rubbing against his organ as well. The slow, serpentine movements began at once, her slender form becoming a long, undulating caress, and the low, soft half-song had begun again before he came to her, slid into her waiting welcome, moved deeply again to rest against the soft inner wall of her dark, wet funnel.

"Fargo . . . uuuummmm . . . uuuummmmmm," Clare sang as once again she turned and twisted with him until the moment erupted and she cried out into his chest once more, clinging to him with arms and legs until she fell back in exhaustion. He let her stay against him until her breathing returned to normal.

"Get back and get some sleep," he ordered.

She nodded obediently, slipped the loose shirt on

as she sat up. She rose, wrapped the blanket around herself, and hurried silently away without another word.

He saw her lie down beside her pack, and he closed his eyes, slept quickly until the morning came in, the wind less warm than the day before. He rose, dressed as Jennifer and Clare still slept. He wandered into the trees, spotted a stand of wild apples, and gathered enough for breakfast. When he returned, Clare was somewhere in the brush washing and Jennifer had just buttoned up the lime blouse.

She spun to face him as he put the apples down, and he saw the anger in her face. "Liar," she flung at him. "But I expected as much."

"What's up your craw?" He frowned.

"I was wakened last night, the sounds hardly mistakable," Jennifer snapped.

"Oh," he grunted, smiled. "I try to satisfy."

"You didn't waste time in proving me right," she said.

"Right about what?"

"About why you brought her along."

Fargo's eyes narrowed a fraction, but Jennifer's anger let her ignore the sign. "I told you she'd be of help. She's already proven that much," he said. "That's all you have to care about, honey."

"And that justifies your playing stud. How convenient," Jennifer threw back.

Fargo let his lips purse. "You know, you sound right jealous," he commented.

Jennifer's face reddened, grew darker than the orange-red hair. "I'm nothing of the kind, and you know it," she half-shouted. "But you didn't bring her to be of help. I know that, and I don't like being lied to."

"Me neither," Fargo said blandly, saw Jennifer's instant frown, a wariness come into the sweet-violet eyes.

"What does that mean?" she asked.

He half-shrugged. "Work on it," he said.

Jennifer's eyes stayed on him, probing, and he saw her decide not to pursue the remark. "I hired you. That's enough. I don't want anyone else involved in chasing Slattery."

"Any special reason?" he questioned.

"I don't need a reason. That's just the way I want it," Jennifer snapped imperiously. "She's half-Indian. You said she knows these mountains. Then she can fend for herself. You send her packing or I will."

Fargo's voice turned harsh. "You keep forgetting something. I call the shots. No arguments, no debates. You forget it one more time, and you can forget about me. Or maybe you want to fire me here and now," he said.

Jennifer glared back as she stayed silent.

"Then have some breakfast and let's hit the trail," Fargo finished. He half-turned away as Clare came through the trees, towel and hairbrush in hand, her jet tresses glistening in the morning sun. She pounced on the apples with a little cry of delight as Jennifer picked two almost disdainfully but bit into the first with hunger.

"Put the rest in your pockets. We'll eat on the way," Fargo said as he saddled the Ovaro.

When he was ready to set out, he saw the mountains offered a trail that was a shallow incline, and he took it at once. Jennifer rode at the rear with the packhorse, he noted, and when the passage widened, Clare brought the gray gelding up alongside him.

"I heard part of it," she said. "She's not happy."

He shrugged off the observation.

"I still say I'm right. She wants you, even if she doesn't know it herself."

"It's not that," he disagreed. "Jennifer wants nothing that'll distract me from chasing Slattery."

"Maybe, but she wants you, too," Clare insisted.

"Jennifer has her mind on cash, not cock," Fargo said.

"One doesn't cancel out the other," Clare returned. "You'll see."

A sudden curl of wind whistled down from the mountain to whirl against his face, and Fargo glanced up. "She might not get either," he grunted, and quickened the pace. He was almost sorry he'd done so when the passage came to an end in a sharp upward climb of jagged rock. His eyes searched the immediate area for another path and found nothing. He cursed softly when he looked at the packhorse as Jennifer came to a halt, let his glance travel up the rock-strewn path again. He couldn't see the end, but he could very well see that there was nothing but rock and more rock, round, smooth, square, jagged. His lips pulled back in distaste as he glanced at the packhorse again. Even with a lightened load, the horse was not built for this kind of climbing. But he was out of choices, Fargo realized grimly. They had to go up. The packhorse would make it or he was done for. He waved his arm forward and started up the steep, rock-filled passage.

He felt the Ovaro slow at once, feel with his hooves for a spot to dig in, pull himself upward. He let the horse set his own pace, find his own places, and he responded each time the Ovaro's feet slipped on a smooth rock, twisted his body in the saddle to help counterbalance. He peered up the steep incline and swore again. The passage stayed the same as far as he could see. He halted the Ovaro, held one arm up to signal a rest, and turned in the saddle. Clare was close enough on the gray gelding, Jennifer back a half-dozen yards with the packhorse. He felt the Ovaro's legs quiver, the resting place not really a resting place, and he moved the horse forward. The Ovaro kept on, suddenly half-leapt forward as his ankle hit a jagged edge of rock, and Fargo was just able to clutch the saddle horn to avoid falling. He glanced back, saw that Clare had watched, and she steered the gelding around the spot. Jennifer had fallen too far back to see, and he halted, waited for her to catch up.

"Look out, just ahead of you," he called as she neared the spot. He saw her eyes widen as she spied the jagged pieces; she pulled her horse to the side and managed to avoid the sharp edges. But the packhorse went into them, reared in pain, and fell onto both foreknees.

Fargo saw the panic in Jennifer's eyes. "Let him alone. Let him get up by himself," he shouted, and she nodded, held her horse in place. Slowly, the packhorse regained its footing and started forward, but Fargo saw the blood streaming down both forelegs and on the fetlock joints.

He cursed and turned the Ovaro upward again, moved on slowly, rested after another ten minutes. The gray gelding's short, sturdy legs were handling the climb well enough, he saw, but Jennifer had fallen back some twenty yards. He watched her cling to her seat as her horse stumbled, fell on one knee, rose up. She kept hold of the lead attached to the packhorse and he watched her arm jerk back as the packhorse slipped, fell, struggled up.

"Damn," Fargo swore as he went on once again. He felt the Ovaro's legs quivering as he used powerful shoulder muscles to pull himself forward instead of pressing down on the rocks that were alternately smooth and jagged. Fargo's mouth almost edged a smile as he spotted the top suddenly, and he fought down the urge to quicken the Ovaro's pace. He kept the reins loose, let the horse continue, felt the horse's right foreleg go down, held his seat in the saddle, and let the horse pull himself upright. Fargo's hand stroked the Ovaro's neck and the top of his shoulder, calmed the horse, and the animal began to pull upward again.

Fargo heard the long drain of a sigh that came from his lips as he reached the top, found a small flat table of land with scattered brush cover. He dismounted, stepped to the edge as Clare came up on the gray gelding and drew the horse to one side. She dropped to the ground, picked up the gelding's forefeet, one after the other. "He's banged up, but he'll get over it with a night's rest," she said.

Fargo heard the rumble of loose rock, the half-cry, half-whinny of a horse, and he spun, peered down the passage. Jennifer had halted some fifteen yards below, and he saw the packhorse behind her struggling to its knees. Under the orange-red hair, Jennifer's loveliness was made of fear and tension as she continued to hold on to the packhorse. Her eyes found Fargo starting down toward her.

"Shall I turn him loose?" she called.

"Christ, no," Fargo roared. "The pull of that lead is the only thing that's keeping him from going down backward." He slid and stumbled down to where she had halted, edged past her, and took the lead to the packhorse. "Go on up," he told Jennifer, pulled steadily on the lead as she moved on.

The packhorse got one leg up and Fargo exerted a firm, steady pressure as he pulled and saw the horse get his other foreleg up. Fargo kept the lead tight as he started to back upward, watching the packhorse's tentative, painful steps. But his firm pressure on the lead helped the horse pull forward and slowly, stumbling, breathing heavily, the horse somehow managed to go on until they reached the top.

Clare moved in to help pull on the lead and the horse struggled onto the flat table of land to stand with legs trembling, bleeding, his breath sucked in with loud wheezing gasps. Fargo used his throwing knife to cut the few packs from the horse, pushed them aside with his foot.

"Divide the stuff three ways," he said to the two young women as he knelt down and examined the horse's legs, his eyes moving from the fetlocks up along the cannon bones to the forearms, up to breastbone and shoulder. His bit out words with quiet anger. "He's finished. Legs pulled to pieces, bone injuries, muscles torn, burst blood vessels," he said, casting an angry glance at Jennifer. "I told you he couldn't cut it up in these mountains. I just didn't figure it would happen this fast," he said.

"Let him go free," Clare said. "He might make it, somehow."

"He's hardly able to walk. The wolves or cougars will make bait of him," Fargo muttered, his eyes hard blue as they touched Jennifer.

"You're blaming me," she said. "That's not fair."

"It's fair as hell. A good horse ruined by expecting the wrong things of him. It always digs at me," he told her.

He saw her swallow. "I'm sorry," she murmured.

"You two go on," Fargo growled. "I'll take care of it and catch up to you." He waited, watched them add the packs to their horses and start up the passage that was gratefully even, mostly dirt and chickweed. He waited till they were out of sight and turned to the horse, whose breathing had come back to normal. The blood running down the animal's forelegs had begun to cake, but it would still be as a beacon to the noses of the big predators in the mountain fastness.

Fargo unholstered the Colt. The act was always one he hated doing, cruelty as mercy, killing to prevent killing. It never really made sense, yet he was all too aware of the thinking behind it. Mercy turned in on itself, he grimaced as he raised the Colt. "Damn," he swore aloud, and his eyes moved over the horse's hindquarters. A few bruises, a little swelling around the stifle, but otherwise all right. Maybe the damn horse could get lucky, find a place to regain strength. Maybe the wolves would be full of elk or deer for a few nights and maybe the mountain lion hunted high ground for the moment. Unlikely, yet not impossible. He lowered the Colt. The horse deserved a chance. Nature made its own decisions, sometimes cruelly, sometimes with surprising mercy. Holstering the Colt, Fargo climbed onto the Ovaro, left the heavy blanket tied across the horse's back. It could help keep a cougar's claws from digging deep.

"Good luck, feller," he murmured as he wheeled the Ovaro and moved on along the pathway, riding slowly, letting the Ovaro go easy on its legs and ankles. He came onto Clare and Jennifer waiting a few hundred yards ahead.

"I didn't hear a shot," Clare remarked.

"That's right," Fargo said, his voice flat. "Everything deserves a chance to live or die on its own." He spurred the pinto forward and heard the two horses behind him start to follow. They rode in silence as the path grew steeper but stayed negotiable, curved, moved closer to the line of maples, grew steeper again, and suddenly he saw the house tucked into the trees.

Jennifer spotted it too and he heard her excited gasp. He put the Ovaro into a trot, halted, and dropped to the ground as the house came into full view. A lean-to more than a cabin, he saw, one half sturdy enough, set back, the other with only a roof and one wall and a canvas second wall. The lean-to was empty, and he entered, Jennifer hurrying up behind him.

His eyes took in a puncheon table, a wood bedstead anchored to the far wall, and a block chair. Two trenchers rested on the table, bits of rabbit bone in one, a few rocklike crumbs of johnnycake on the table. Weeks old, he estimated by the layer of dust over everything.

"He was here," Jennifer said excitedly as she went over the lean-to.

"Somebody was here," Fargo said.

"No, it was him . . . Slattery," Jennifer said, new excitement catching her voice. "Here's proof." She picked up a little piece of green-dyed paper. "This is part of the outside wrapping of the tobacco he smokes, Old Bull Root," she said. "He was here. We're on the right trail."

Fargo glanced outside at the sky, a soft rose as the sun moved behind the mountains to end the day. "We'll bed down here for the night," he said, spotted a splint broom in one corner of the lean-to. "Sweep the dust out of here while I unsaddle the horses," he said. He stepped outside, halted at the side of the passage that had brought them to the lean-to, and his eyes slowly swept the canopy of trees on all sides. Half the leaves had fallen, he guessed, and it was becoming easier to see into the thick woods. Satisfied that nothing dangerous moved out there, he unsaddled the horses, finished as dark descended. He returned to the lean-to to find Jennifer's gaze on him. "I'll bed down outside," he said, and saw her face set at once.

"Of course," she bit out tartly, slapped her blanket down on the bedstead.

Clare put her things in the opposite corner and Fargo broke out a tin of the beef and some of the hardtack. "We'll look at the map come morning," he said as he ate quickly, finished, rose to his feet. He stretched and his back reminded him of the grueling climb up the rock passage. The two young women not more than dark shadows now, he picked up his things and went outside, walked a half-dozen yards from the ramshackle structure, and set his things down under the low branches of a low dwarf maple.

He undressed to his shorts, positioned the big Colt beside the bedroll, and lay down as the night wind grew sharper, developed the edge of frost in it. He heard the sound of distant wolves, listened to them move farther away, down the mountains. The big gray predators preferred the lower mountains and seldom moved high up the forbidding slopes. He lay quietly, letting tired muscles relax when he heard the soft steps, padded feet, almost noiseless, betrayed only by the dry fall leaves that littered the ground. He half-turned to see the broad head nearby, the white, tufted sideburns of the lynx, and he watched the animal leap effortlessly onto a low branch, pause, and disappear down the other side. A big, formidable specimen, he took note, a silent reminder that danger and death were never far away in the fastness of the great mountains.

He lay back, sloed his eyes, and waited, finally felt himself falling asleep. But his ears caught the sound of quick steps and he snapped his eyes open, saw Clare hurrying to him, clad only in the loose over-size shirt. He moved over inside the bedroll and Clare almost leapt in beside him as he felt her skin chilled in only the few yards she'd crossed to reach him. "I'd about given up on you," he said as he pressed the warmth of his body over her.

"I waited for her to fall asleep," Clare said.

"Being modest?" he asked in some surprise.

"Being kind," she said.

He stroked her face with his hand. "You've a good heart, Clare," he said.

"A lot of good other things, too," she murmured, pulled the shirt from herself, and he felt her legs lift, open, clasp around him. "God, I've been waiting all day for this moment," she breathed.

He felt the almost smooth nap rub against him, the little mound rising to press against his expanding, ballooning maleness that found its own way at once into the waiting warmth of her. "Mmmmm . . . oh . . . oh, mmmmm," she crooned, and he heard the half-moan, half-song begin again deep inside her. Her arms closed around the back of his neck, pulled his mouth down onto her breasts, each little erect nipple almost quivering, waiting, pushing for his lips, the caress of his tongue.

Her slender body turned and twisted and writhed in the sinuous movements that were her lovemaking, and once again, when the moment rushed upon her, she rose to cling against him, legs clasped high around the small of his back, her pelvis thrust tight against him as little spasms coursed through her and she moaned into his chest. When she fell back, depleted, her legs continued to stay clasped around him, and he rubbed the little mound under the thin, almost flat black triangle until she finally let her legs fall open and she rolled to come against him, stay child-like in his arms.

"Can I stay here?" she murmured.

"We'd neither get much sleep, I'm thinking," he said gently. "And the riding gets harder each day."

She nodded, rose, a half-pout touching her face, and her fingers caressed the handsome, chiseled line of his jaw. "You're right, of course, damn you," she said, and pulled the oversize shirt on. She pressed lips to him quickly, a dart of her tongue as a reminder, and then she hurried back to the lean-to. He watched till she disappeared inside, then he pulled the bed-roll around himself and slept quickly. The trip was having unexpected rewards. Maybe luck would ride all the way with him, he murmured silently as sleep washed away further thoughts.

4

The morning came with a touch of frost and a touch of fire. The frost arrived with the north wind that whipped down from the high peaks. The fire came out of the lean-to. Fargo had just finished dressing when he heard Jennifer's voice, first, rising angrily.

"Slut," she said, the single word wreathed in contempt.

"Bitch," he heard Clare fire back.

The sound of the slap echoed as though it were a distant shot, followed by another, and he heard Jennifer's gasp, then her cry of fury mingled with Clare's deeper curses.

"Shit," Fargo swore as he raced for the lean-to, leapt inside, and saw Jennifer using height and weight to bend Clare backward over the edge of the bedstead. Clare pulled hard on a handful of orange-red hair. He reached the clawing, panting, cursing forms in one long stride, grasped flailing arms, yanked Jennifer back first, sent her reeling into one corner of the lean-to and flung Clare into the other.

"Goddamn," he swore at both.

"She started it," Clare said. "Calling me names."

"She asked for it," Jennifer flung back, violet eyes blazing.

"Take that map of yours and go outside. I'll talk to you there," Fargo ordered angrily. Jennifer's glance at Clare was pure venom as she took the leather pouch and stormed from the lean-to. His glance at

Clare was harsh. "You stay here and be quiet," he ordered. Clare's eyes held a hint of sullenness.

He turned from her and strode outside to where Jennifer had the map in her hand. "The map, first," he barked, taking it from her. His eyes scanned the piece of paper and saw the next mark on it indicated a cabin halfway up to the timberline. No trails noted, he cursed silently, only signposts and a few scrawled arrows marking a general direction. But Slattery's plan was coming clear in a kind of roundabout way, and Fargo frowned in thought as he peered at the map. He raised his eyes to Jennifer. "Was Slattery working with your pa most of the time before he ran off with the money?" he asked.

"Pretty much so," she answered. "Except for a few days here and there." She studied his face, frowned. "Why?"

"Then he didn't have time to prepare to hole up for the winter. That'd take a whole summer of preparing. He's planned to hide out till the first snows and then make his way down," Fargo said, but his frown deepened as the next thought pushed at him. "But he wasn't running just from your pa, not this high up in the mountains. He expected somebody else coming after him, this Davis character, probably," Fargo said.

"I wouldn't know about that," Jennifer said blandly.

Fargo handed the map back to her as his eyes hardened. "As for that business just now, I don't want any more of it," he growled.

Jennifer flared at once. "It's bad enough without her pushing it at me," she said. " 'Sleep well?' she asked me." Jennifer's voice lowered a half-octave as she imitated Clare. " 'I slept wonderfully, real satisfied,' " she mimicked.

"Then you started to call names," Fargo said.

Jennifer shrugged away his words. "She deserved it."

Fargo's words shot at her as though they were

bullets. "No more, dammit. No more name-calling, no more digs, no more anything, you hear me? What she does is her business, not yours."

Jennifer's eyes took on a lavender veil of stubborn anger. "I don't want her around. I don't care if she can help," Jennifer said.

"I care, and you damn well better listen to what I said," he tossed back.

Jennifer glowered at him as he turned and strode into the lean-to.

Clare's eyes were cool and contained as she met his glare.

"You pushed it at her, she told me. Why? What happened to being kind?" he asked in honest bewilderment.

"Changed my mind," Clare tossed back.

"Goddamn," Fargo breathed as he shook his head. "There's no damn understanding a woman."

Clare suddenly flared. "She's got no right to look at me as if I'm some kind of dirt," she said. "I told you, the world doesn't hold a whole lot of joy when you don't fit anywhere, but I'm not taking any more of that kind of thing. No more, not from anybody."

Fargo felt the rush of understanding for her spiral through him, and he reached out, touched her face. "All right, no more names from her, no more sideways digging from you. Any more of it and I leave you both high and dry here," he said.

"Your leaving scares me, nothing else," Clare said as she leaned her head against his chest. "You're the only good thing that's come my way in too long a time."

He held her for a moment, then pushed her away. "Then mind your tongue," he snapped, and strode from the lean-to. "Saddle up," he called outside. "Let's get moving." He watched Jennifer and Clare studiously ignore each other as they readied themselves to leave. When he finished saddling the Ovaro and strapping on a third of what the packhorse had

84

carried, he saw both women waiting, watching him. His eyes held on Clare. "The map marks a place with the name of Sounding Rocks," he said. "Ever hear of it?"

Clare frowned, reached back in her memory. "Not by that name. That's a white man's name," she said, her brow staying furrowed. "There was somewhere, my mother used to talk about it once in a while, a spot the Indians call the Place of the Singing Stones."

"Close enough. You remember where it was?" Fargo questioned.

She pointed up and north to a white-capped peak. "That way. I remember my mother saying it was a hard place to reach."

He made a wry sound. "What isn't hard up here?" he said. "Let's move."

He set off at a careful pace. The load the packhorse had carried had been divided and each horse carried added weight now. He let the Ovaro pretty much set his own pace and found a stretch of red and black currants that made good eating as they rode. By midafternoon he felt the tiredness of horse and riders as the continued upward climb became grueling. He felt the frustration mirrored in Jennifer's face at the slowness of their progress, and when he spotted a pack of snowshoe hares, he pulled the Sharps from its case, took aim, and brought down a big buck hare. "It's time we had some fresh meat for dinner," he said as he tied the hare to his saddlebag.

The night began to close in as he found himself at the edge of a series of gentle hills set into the giant craggy peaks, thickly covered with Norway spruce and balsam fir. He stared at the terrain with the welcome a starving man gives to the sight of food. He made camp under a thick panoply of protective spruce branches as the darkness slipped over the land. He set Jennifer to building a small fire as he skinned the rabbit and then fashioned a roasting spit from a piece of thin branch. He moved his own bedroll deep into the pine-scented woods, saw Jennifer hold her disapproval in her eyes as he returned to the fire. The hare, when thoroughly roasted, became a small feast of succulent dining, and when it was finished, Jennifer was first to undress and climb under her blanket. Fargo smothered the fire, and the chill of the night wind rushed into the vacuum where warmth had kept it at bay.

The cold stabbed at him as he undressed and slid into his bedroll, and when the moon rose high, Clare came wrapped in her blanket. Her lovemaking held a fervid intensity, a passionate urgency beyond anything it had held before, as though she tried to erase this morning's displeasure with her body. Whatever the reason, he found a new height of pleasure in her slender, coiled fervency, and when he finally lay alone, he slept soundly until the morning light.

Jennifer greeted him with tight-lipped silence and eyes of violet steel—but nothing else, her thoughts held to herself in silence. "Very good," he muttered as she passed him in the cotton nightdress. She ignored his remark and disappeared into the trees to dress. When she returned, Clare was ready also, and he led the way through the pine-covered gentle hills, grateful for the easy-riding terrain. The thick Norway spruce and balsam were joined by heavy growths of the shorter black spruce, and he threaded a path through the trees. A tiny brook let the horses drink cool, clear water, and Fargo's eyes peered up into the canopy of pine boughs. The chill of the air stayed and made him grimace.

It was midafternoon and they had reached deep into the vast stand of pine and spruce when he reined up sharply, motioned for silence. He strained his ears, which had picked up the whinny of a horse, discerned the sound again, and he slid to the ground to go forward on foot. When he sank to one knee behind the thick boughs of a black spruce, Clare and Jennifer came up behind him, followed his gaze at the figures almost directly ahead of them, most wearing deerskin capes, and browbands as they sat their pinto ponies. Fargo counted eight, including the one that wore a single eagle feather in his hair, which marked him as the leader. The Trailsman glanced at Clare, motioned to their moccasins with his eyes, and she nodded at the geometric pattern of red against blue-dyed background.

"Arapaho," she whispered in confirmation. Jennifer's lavender orbs were wide with apprehension as Fargo drew back, retreated to where he'd left the horses.

"Run for it?" Jennifer asked.

He shook his head. "They'd hear us. They're too close. They'd be on us in minutes."

"They're coming this way. They'll be on us anyway in minutes," Jennifer answered.

Fargo felt the muscles in his neck throbbing. "Fade back, slow, quiet," he said grimly. "We've got to buy some thinking time." He moved his horse back through the woods as he half-whispered the thoughts that raced through his mind like so many runaway tops spinning wildly. "Can't outrun them, not through these trees, not with them this close," he murmured. "Can't outfight them here, either. Got to find something to turn them away, keep them from hitting us."

"We could give them something, maybe," Jennifer said. "Our blankets? Something they could use?"

Fargo frowned at her as thoughts suddenly exploded inside him. "They've better blankets than we have," he said, but the single thought that had struck fire began to grow. His eyes went to Clare, saw her watching him as she picked up his thinking. "Mountain man," he said, and she nodded.

"What do you mean?" Jennifer asked.

"Mountain men have a special place. The Indians usually let them alone. They're no threat and they're

87

usually as wild as the Indians," Fargo said, his eyes staying on Clare.

"Especially if they have an Indian wife," she added, her gaze steady. She slipped from her horse, began to twirl her fingers through her jet tresses to braid them, and Fargo turned his eyes to Jennifer.

"I'm going to play mountain man and Clare's going to be my Arapaho wife," he said. "If we can pull it off, we might just walk away in one piece."

"Where does that leave me?" Jennifer asked.

"You'll be a captive, a slave girl with your wrists tied," he said.

Jennifer's eyes shot violet fire at once. "Why can't she be the slave girl and I be your wife?" she demanded.

Fargo's voice edged impatience. "Because if you and I are dragging along an Arapaho slave girl, you can be damn sure they'll lift our scalps," he said.

Jennifer fell silent, her lips pressed down on each other.

"Now give me your wrists and I'll tie you up," Fargo said, and she extended her arms with a reluctant glower. "Stay looking unhappy," he said. "It'll help the picture."

He looped a length of lariat around her wrists and tied her to the saddle horn on her horse. With a quick motion, he pulled her shirt loose and tore it up one side to expose a length of cream-white skin and part of the side of one full breast. "What's that for, dammit?" she hissed.

"Can't have you all nice and neat. Won't look right," he said, and he saw uncertain skepticism in the lavender orbs. His gaze went to Clare as she stepped forward, her black hair hanging in two braids. The effect was remarkable as she suddenly looked very Indian, the planes of her face taking on new aspects. He watched as she reached into her saddle-bag and rummaged, came out with a deerskin dress cut in the Arapaho style with the uneven edge along the top band. She slipped it over her head and the transformation was complete and startling. Even her dark-blue eyes seemed almost brown.

"It was my mother's," she said. "I've kept it all these years, but I never thought I'd be wearing it, not like this." She climbed onto the gray gelding and brought the horse alongside him. He took the reins of Jennifer's mount and brought her up behind them. She continued to look sullen and unhappy, he saw with satisfaction as he turned the Ovaro, moved forward in a slow walk. The row of Indians materialized through the trees in but a few minutes, and he saw two immediately move out as flankers as the others moved straight toward him.

He reined up as the line of horsemen halted across his path. He saw their faces stay hard as they took in the big man and the two women.

The one with the lone eagle feather in his hair moved toward them, and the others started to encircle the three riders. Tall, a strong nose with a scar along the bridge of it, the Arapaho halted again and his black glittering eyes took in Clare, moved to Jennifer, paused at her orange-red hair, and returned to Fargo. "Mountain man?" the Indian asked.

The Arapaho spoke the Algonquian language, and Fargo knew enough for a short conversation. He let his eyes meet the Indian's gaze as he nodded. He watched the Arapaho's eyes slowly travel over his horse, the saddle, the extra packs tied on behind the cantle.

"No traps," the Indian observed, and his black eyes grew smaller.

Fargo started to motion to the canvas-wrapped packs and changed his mind. If the Arapaho insisted on seeing them, he'd be caught in a lie and the whole game would be over. Besides, the Mountain men most always carried their traps out in plain view. He pointed up higher into the mountains and made the sign for digging into the earth to say that his traps were set out.

The Indian accepted his answer and let his eyes rest on Clare. "You mountain man's wife?" he asked her, and she nodded, kept her eyes downcast respectfully.

The Arapaho grunted and moved his pony a few paces sideways, rested his eyes on Jennifer. He pointed at her as he spoke to Fargo. "You buy?" he asked.

Fargo shook his head. "I take," he said, and the Indian's eyes flickered in the immobile face. Fargo felt the tiny beads of perspiration trickling down the back of his neck as he kept his own face expressionless. The Arapaho's eyes moved over the Ovaro, circled the horse slowly, obvious appreciation coming into the black, glittering eyes. Fargo held the sigh inside himself. Part of the game had been won. The Arapaho leader had accepted the mountain-man charade, but there would have to be payment for the privilege of being allowed to go on. Normally it would be a prize skin or beaver pelts, but there were none to offer. He watched as the Indian raised his arm, pointed at the Ovaro.

Fargo shook his head. The Arapaho pointed at the Ovaro again. He wanted the horse, but it was also an opening bid. The Indians were inveterate bargainers, not just with the white man. They bargained among themselves constantly. But there were rituals to it that had to be observed. Bargaining was one thing. Refusal another. The Arapaho had made his demand and had been turned down, made it again with the same result. He sat back on his pony now and waited, his face stone.

It was his turn, Fargo knew, up to him to make a counteroffer. But it had to be of substance, or it would be taken as an insult and everything would blow up in his face. Fargo met the Arapaho's black eyes, which told him nothing, and once again he felt the trickle of perspiration down his neck.

He turned, pointed to Jennifer, and saw her eyes widen, her lips drop open.

"What are you doing?" she gasped out.

Fargo didn't answer, watched the Indian's eyes move over her again, obvious appreciation in the black orbs. But he had to be faithful to the bargaining ritual. He pointed to the Ovaro again. Fargo pointed to Jennifer.

"No, dammit, what do you think you're doing?" Jennifer half-shouted at him, panic seizing her eyes. "He wants your horse, dammit," she said.

"And I'm giving him you, instead," Fargo rasped. Clare sat silently, eyes downcast, playing her role perfectly. He saw fury push the panic out of Jennifer's eyes.

"You can't. You wouldn't," she breathed.

He looked away from her, his eyes on the Indian. The Arapaho moved his horse closer to Jennifer and his hand reached out, brushed the orange-red hair. She tried to pull away, but her wrists, tied to the saddle horn, held her in place. Fargo saw the Arapaho smile as his eyes devoured her hair, went down to the torn shirt where the side of one full white breast was plainly in view. He reached out again, took the horse's reins this time, and slowly started to lead the horse in a circle. Fargo felt the deep breath escape his lips. It was done with, the bargain made. He stayed in place as the Arapaho led Jennifer away and saw her half-turn in the saddle, the consuming rage still keeping panic out of her eyes.

"You bastard," she screamed. "You rotten, stinking bastard." Fargo sat motionless as the Arapahos began to fade into the trees. "Don't do this to me," he heard Jennifer's voice screaming, fear coming into her cries now. "Fargo, don't. You son of a bitch, Fargo," she shouted, alternating between fear and fury. Her screams died away as the Arapaho continued on. Fargo let his shoulders slump, pushed his hat back, and wiped the perspiration from his neck. He felt Clare's eyes on him, a long, unsmiling stare.

"You're going back to get her," she said, her voice flat.

"That's right," he answered. "You didn't think I was just going to ride on, did you really?" He frowned.

She shrugged and the gesture surprised him. He saw the veil slide over her eyes. "You think you can do it?" she asked.

"Night, surprise, all the little things on my side this time," he said.

"You could still lose your scalp," she said.

"I'll try not to," he said dryly.

"She worth it?" Clare slid out. "You're not sure of her story. She could be lying to you about everything. Why bother with her?"

"Worth has nothing to do with it. I put her neck into it. Had no choice, but I still did it. I owe her a chance to get out," he said.

"I don't. She's not worth my scalp, her and her high and mighty ways," Clare snapped.

He felt surprise at the depth of her anger. A very real, very female personal dislike, its own brand of jealousy mixed in, and something more, a vast reservoir of resigned bitterness.

"You working on a case of divided loyalties?" he pushed at her.

She paused before answering. "No, I didn't interest them. They knew I wasn't full-blooded Arapaho. I don't have any loyalties, divided or any other kind. I don't fit anywhere, I told you," she said.

He watched as she slid from the gray gelding, pulled the deerskin dress over her head, folded it carefully, and put it back in the saddlebag, investing the act with a silent statement.

"You'll go after her on your own," she muttered, not looking at him.

92

"Don't remember asking for help," he said, not ungently.

She turned, put her back to him. "Light's fading. You want to pick up their trail, you better get started," she said.

"You're right," he said, and nudged the Ovaro into a slow walk. He passed her, kept on, started to move into the pines.

Her voice broke the silence. "Fargo!" she called, and he halted, looked back at her. "If they'd taken me, would you be going after me?" she asked, and in the question lay all the bitterness, hope, and hurt that was inside her.

But he refused to feed into it and his voice was hard. "Answer that for yourself," he barked, turned, and rode into the trees.

The trail was easy to pick up, even in the dim light that had begun to infuse the thick-boughed pine forest. The Arapaho hadn't hurried. They'd no reason to, and the eagle-feather warrior wouldn't bother Jennifer, not much, at least, not until he could bring her to the main camp and show her off first.

Fargo followed their trail until he suddenly reined up, the light still gray in the forest. He smelled smoke, sniffed again, caught the scent of pine branches burning. They had made an early camp, which meant that the main camp lay somewhere down in the lower mountains, far enough away to make it another day's ride.

Fargo pulled back, retreated in the last of the light. He'd leave plenty of distance between him and the Arapaho. The smoke would mark their location and he didn't want a shift in the sharp night wind bringing the scent of saddle leather to them. He dismounted, stretched out on a soft bed of pine needles, and watched the grayness fade into the deep black of night. He lay relaxed, arms behind his head, half-dozed, immersed in the blackness. The moon had begun to rise, not high enough yet to allow more than a glimmer of pale light through the thick boughs, when he snapped awake at the sound, the big Colt in his hand at once. He listened, picked up the soft, slow, steady sound of a horse being walked carefully. He rose, eyes narrowed, positioned himself behind the trunk of a thick Norway spruce. The direction of the sound made him all but certain who was approaching, yet he wasn't one to take chances. He waited till the dark form of the horse and rider came into view, moving slowly through the trees.

He stepped forward and saw her start in surprise. She swung down from the horse to stand in front of him, met his narrowed gaze. "I thought she wasn't worth your scalp," he said.

"She isn't. You are," Clare answered solemnly. Her arms lifted, came around his neck. "How far away are they?" she murmured.

"Far enough," he said as he sank down onto the soft pine needles with her. She had pulled her shirt off before his head lay against the bed of pine, her lips pressing his, a harsh, demanding pressure.

"Do it like it might never be again," she said, words impossible to brush aside.

He felt her fear and urgency transmit themselves to him, the desire given new, sudden impetus. Her hands closed around him and she gasped as she stroked the pulsing, throbbing wanting of him. He shed remaining clothes with her, and her slender legs rubbed up and down his body before they fell open to encircle him, clasp tight around him as she drew him into her. The moaning song began again, but this time it was caught up with a turbulent insistence, stronger, almost a harshness in it.

"Fargo," she whispered against him, "now, now, now." He slid into her and felt her shudder, pull against him, and he rolled onto his back with her. She pressed forward, pushed the modest breasts into his face, the pink-brown tips seeking his mouth. He took them in, first one, then the other, and she

94

began to pump her hips atop him, plunging herself down on him as far as she could go, pressing the inner wall of her against his swollen, pulsing organ as she gave tiny little gasps. She rode atop him as though she were upon a bucking stallion, rising up, plunging down, and each time the gasped cry came from her. "Agh . . . agh . . . aiii . . . ah, ah, ah . . . ah, oh, God," she breathed, and he was first to feel her legs grow tight, stiffen, caught the rising climax of her before she felt it. He reached up, pulled her to him, rolled again, and was atop her as she screamed, drove her pubic mound hard against him, held it there to quiver and tremble as he came with her and saw her neck arch backward, her entire body lift, hang in midair until she fell back, her hands digging into his shoulders. "Mmmm . . . oh . . . ooooh," she breathed as he stayed inside her, felt the last little contractions slowly subside.

She finally let him pull from her, lay against him. "This is the only place I've ever fitted, Fargo, with you, beside you, you inside me," she murmured, and he held her close, let her grow still, rest, until he glimpsed the moon through the boughs over their heads.

She stirred at his touch.

"Time to go," he said, and slid his body from the warmth of her arms, pushed himself to his feet and dressed.

Clare sat up, awake at once, pulled on clothes. She moved forward beside him as he led the Ovaro through the spruce.

The Arapaho fire had died out, but the strong odor of smoldering pine branches hung in the air, acted as an invisible beacon. He followed the scent, glimpsed a small half-circle amid the trees, and halted, his eyes slowly traveling over the sleeping figures. "Damn," he murmured to Clare, who was kneeling beside him. "They're sleeping too far apart." Her frown questioned. "If they were close together, a

95

volley could take out five or six at once," he explained. "This way you'll have to draw a bead on each one you shoot. You wouldn't get more than two or three before the others woke."

He swept the half-circle again, his lips drawn back in distaste. Of course it was no coincidence that the Arapaho slept separated as they did. A volley of arrows could be as deadly as a volley of bullets. His gaze halted at the figure on the far side, hair a dull red in the faint light. He saw that they'd left her wrists tied and bound her ankles. Rawhide thongs, most likely, he grunted. He turned options in his mind. Taking out most in one surprise attack was no longer one of them. That left two things only. "We've got to slip her out without waking them and stop them from coming after us," he said to Clare.

"Run their horses?" she whispered back.

"Tricky business that," he said. "Take perfect timing. The horses running off will have them all up instantly. We've got to be ready to hightail it at the same moment."

"You see to her. I'll run the horses," Clare said. Fargo continued to ponder. "What is it?" Clare asked.

"Hobbling their horses would keep them off our tail without us having to time it perfectly," he said, turned the thought in his mind again. He had started to discard it and Clare's comment added to the decision.

"Hobbling eight horses would take time," she said.

"Too much time," he agreed. "Too much could go wrong. We'll have to run them and hope we can pull it off." He rose, started to move in a circle around the still campsite, leading the Ovaro as Clare led the gray. He moved slowly, kept a wide arc around the half-circle, and finally halted as they came to where the Indian ponies were tethered together on a single long line. "Move in easy, wait till I have her untied," he said.

She nodded and he took the gray gelding's reins

from her, led the horse around the Indian ponies along with the Ovaro until he was at the other side of them. He moved in closer to the half-circle and the sleeping figures, then draped the reins over a low branch and, in a low crouch, stepped out of the trees. He swept the Arapaho with another quick glance, took one long stride, and dropped to one knee beside Jennifer. She half-turned in restless sleep, and he put his hand over her mouth, saw her eyes come open, stare up at him.

"Surprise," he breathed, put one finger to his lips as he took his hand away. He pulled the double-edged throwing knife from the thin leather holster around his calf and cut her wrist bonds. She sat up. The leather thongs around her ankles took more time and he cast another glance at the sleeping figures as he sawed at the bonds. He couldn't see Clare, but he knew she was with the Indian ponies, crouched down, her eyes on him. He cursed silently as the rawhide thongs proved stubbornly strong, pressed harder, and finally felt the incision break the leather apart. The thongs tore open reluctantly, but they finally parted and he stood up, pulled Jennifer to her feet. He waved his arm in the air as he started into the trees where he'd left the Ovaro and the gelding.

His glance had just flicked to the Indian ponies as he heard the short cry of surprise and pain, Clare's voice. He saw her go down as one of the ponies whirled, slammed into her with its rump, then raced away with the others. "Shit," he swore as he also saw the sleeping figures sit up almost as one. He pushed Jennifer into the trees, saw Clare getting up, racing toward him. But the Arapaho were on their feet, shouting curses as they realized their ponies had been run off. He saw two spot him as he ran into the trees, their shouts instant. He reached the Ovaro, half-pushed, half-flung Jennifer into the saddle as Clare ran toward him. He turned, saw the two Arapaho had been joined by two more, racing into the trees at him.

Clare vaulted onto the gray gelding. "Get out of here," he yelled, slapped the Ovaro hard on the rump, and the horse streaked away. He saw Clare hesitate, start to pull back on the gelding to let him leap on, but the Arapaho were there, one veering off to seize the gray's cheek strap.

"Go, dammit," he yelled, and Clare sent the horse streaking forward as the Indian leapt for its head, missed by inches, and fell sprawling on the ground.

Fargo flung himself backward as the other three Arapaho rushed him, and he saw all had tomahawks in hand. He landed on his shoulder, rolled, heard a tomahawk thud into the ground beside him. He snapped the big Colt .45 from its holster, fired at almost-point-blank range at two of the Indians diving at him. Both forms erupted in geysers of red as they fell forward, dropped on each side of him. He saw the third Arapaho coming at him from the left while the fourth ducked behind a tree. Fargo whirled as the third brave came at him in a low, running crouch. He fired and the bullet tore a path through the top of the man's head. The thick, greased black hair was suddenly a dirty red, and the Indian staggered forward, not unlike a chicken with its head cut off, made a half-circle, staggered again, and then dropped to twitch a moment more and lie still.

Fargo caught the soft whoosh of air to his left, dropped as the hunting knife streaked at him. The knife grazed the top of his hat as he hit the ground; he rolled, avoided the Indian's diving leap. He brought the Colt up to fire, had to fall back as the Arapaho swung a tomahawk in a short, flat arc. As he flipped backward to avoid the blow, the Indian leapt up, came at him with the tomahawk raised to strike again. Fargo fired from on his back, the shot through the man's abdomen and out the other side of his body, shattering his spine. The Indian uttered a strange, almost howling sound as he half-turned in midair, collapsed with his body still twisted.

Fargo leapt to his feet as he saw two more figures racing through the trees toward him. The last two had gone after the ponies. Fargo backpedaled. He had two bullets left in the Colt before having to reload. He saw one of the two Arapaho halt, raise his arms, and bring the short, powerful bow up. Fargo flung himself sideways behind a tree as the arrow whistled past him. He peered out, gun high to fire, but the Indian had disappeared. So had the other one. He pulled back, listened, but they were moving on silent feet, huntsmen of consummate skill. He sank down beside the tree for a moment, put four bullets into the Colt, and rose, ears straining, and he picked up the soft sound to his right.

He edged around the tree trunk when he caught the movement of brush behind him, and he spung to see the Arapaho, arrow on the bowstring, directly in front of him. He had a split second to try and dive aside or fire. He elected to fire, brought the Colt up, and pressed the trigger. The bullet caught the Arapaho full in the chest, but he had released the arrow and Fargo saw the shaft streaking at him. He tried to twist away, but it was too late and he felt the breath-catching pain as the arrow slammed into him just below the point of his shoulder. He gasped out as he sank down on one knee, cursed under his breath at wrong decisions.

The Arapaho lay dead, but he'd left his mark. Fargo caught the footsteps to the right of the tree, the other Indian circling around to come at him from the side. Fargo grimaced in pain as the arrow rubbed into torn flesh inside him. There were still two others, the ones that had gone after the ponies. He couldn't afford missed shots now, nor the time for cat-and-mouse games. He slid down, turned onto his side, the Colt pressed into the ground in his hand, and he let his legs hang limply. He lay as if dead, and the

Indian, coming from the side, would only see the feathered end of the arrow sticking into him. He lay motionless, not breathing, and he heard the Arapaho approach, steps quickening. He felt the Indian reach him, grasp his hair with one hand, start to pull him up and around. He kept his body limp, let the Arapaho turn him, and as he came onto his back, the Colt exploded in two shots into the man's groin. Fargo saw the Indian's eyes grow wide in surprise and agony, the hunting knife fall from his hand as he clapped both hands to his groin. Fargo scuttled backward as the Indian fell forward onto both knees, hung there almost as if in prayer, and then toppled onto his face. A slow pool of red oozed from underneath the Arapaho as Fargo pulled himself to his feet.

The Trailsman leaned against the tree for a moment as the shaft protruded from him. Lips drawn back in pain, he grasped the arrow where it had entered his body, broke it off, and gasped at the pain, stayed against the tree a few moments longer, and then pushed himself forward. He started through the trees, a long, half-crouched walk, grimacing against the pain he felt with each step. He'd gone perhaps a few dozen yards when he halted, saw the dark shape standing still beside a black spruce. He moved toward it and the shape became Jennifer's horse, standing quietly, saddle on, reins trailing the ground. He'd been tethered with the Indian ponies, plainly, and ran off as they fled. But he'd gone in another direction on his own and, thoroughly saddle-trained, had halted soon. Fargo reached up with his left arm, got his hand around the saddle horn, and pulled himself onto the horse as he felt the sudden rush of pain from his shoulder. He moved the horse on, tried a trot, and almost screamed with the pain that shot through him. He slowed the horse to a walk at once and made his way back through the pine woods.

He cursed again as he rode. The damn arrowhead continued to tear at flesh and sinew inside his shoulder, a steady, ever-increasing pain, starting to burn into him now. Clare and Jennifer had halted somewhere, he was certain. Could he reach them? he had to wonder as he felt a weakness sliding over him. The arrowhead rested against something that made him tremble—a nerve ending probably—sent waves of increasing weakness through him. The pain he could fight. The trembling and weakness came in waves, impossible to steel himself against. He rode through the faint moonlight and felt sure he was retracing steps. He kept on and cursed the trembling in his right side, which was almost constant now. He was spilling blood, too, he knew, and swore again. If the last two Arapaho decided to follow, they'd have an easy time of it.

He was riding with head bowed, clinging to the saddle horn, trembling harder, as the moonlight faded into the first gray of dawn. He slowed as he spotted the tiny brook and, beyond it, the heavy stand of Norway spruce. He was almost back where he'd started, he saw. He wanted to feel elation but he felt only weakness. He squinted. Something moved up ahead. He tried to straighten, grimaced with the pain of it. His hand went to his Colt as he saw the two horses come into view, break into a gallop toward him. He glimpsed the flash of orange-red hair as he fell forward in the saddle, closed his eyes, his face resting against the Ovaro's warm, powerful neck.

5

He woke and the trembling was still on him. But he was on his back, pine boughs overhead, and the pain had grown more intense. He saw Jennifer first, kneeling at his side, a flash of orange-red, and then Clare came into focus. They had pulled him from his horse, bedded him down on a blanket, and taken his shirt off. He felt a wave of trembling sweep over him again and he waited till it lessened, found his voice. It sounded strange, unsteady.

"Arrowhead's got to come out. It's pressing on a nerve," he said.

"Got to get you back down to a doctor for that," Clare said.

"Never make it," he said. "Never." He paused, gathered words with an effort. "My throwing knife. Thin, double-edged blade. Calf holster," he murmured. He felt Clare's hand reach down his leg and draw the thin, razor-sharp blade from its holster. Again he squeezed words out in clusters as the pain seemed to consume his body. "Cut . . . along shaft. Get to arrowhead, cut along one side. Get it loose . . . pull it out."

He saw Jennifer blanch. "The pain will be terrible," she said.

He disagreed with his eyes. "Knife's very sharp. Cut quick," he said. He saw Clare nod, rise to both knees, and come closer; she bent over his chest, the narrow blade firmly in her hand. He steeled himself as best he could and watched as she lay the thin blade against the broken tip of the shaft, measured, pulled her lips back, and made the first cut, a quick, sharp stroke. She followed instantly with the others, against the edge of the shaft, strokes so sharp he felt only an instant of pain with each.

Jennifer pressed a towel to his chest to catch the blood that ran from the incisions. He felt Clare reach the arrowhead, cut again along one of the triangular sides with the same quick, incisive strokes, and the pain was mercifully brief. But the trembling swept over him, weakening, exhausting as she stopped, her eyes going to his face.

"I've got it free, but it won't come out easy. I'll have to pull," she said.

"Fire first," he breathed. "A branch . . . burn the end of it," he murmured.

He saw Clare turn to Jennifer. "Move," she snapped. "For when the shaft is out. Burning the wound will slow the bleeding and cauterize it. It's got to be done."

"My God," Jennifer muttered as she turned away, began to get a fire started. Clare rolled a kerchief, offered it to him, and he bit down on it, clamped his jaws as hard as he could. Jennifer returned to press both hands down on his shoulders to keep him flat on his back, and he felt Clare move the arrowhead, wriggle it, and slip her fingers into his flesh under the stone. She yanked, down and sideways, along the incision she'd made, and he heard his scream of pain through clenched jaws around the kerchief. A wave of nausea swept over him, the world fading away, growing blurred. He heard Clare's voice as a dim sound.

"It's out, I've got it," she said. He heard Jennifer's voice and the world swam back into focus. He saw Jennifer had the piece of branch in her hand, one end glowing hot. Clare stared at it. "I can't," she murmured. "Not that. I can't."

"Got to," he said, gasping, but Clare drew back and he saw Jennifer rush forward, her face rigid, the glowing branch held low. She almost rushed at him, as if an instant's delay would shatter her courage. She plunged the searing, glowing end of the branch into the wound, half-turned it once, and he heard his scream again, this time no kerchief to deaden the sound. His head fell back and once more the world swam away, became a void.

Slowly, the void became substance again and his eyelids flickered, opened. He smelled the odor of his own charred flesh and he managed to focus his gaze. Jennifer came into view, on her knees, her eyes closed, and she seemed to be holding herself together. Clare, nearby, stared at him.

"My saddlebag," he managed to breathe. "Little jar . . . hyssop and comfrey mix . . . put it on . . . lots of it." He fell back, the effort exhausting, and his eyes closed again. Dimly, he was aware of soft hands rubbing the cool, soothing salve on his wound. Sensation faded away and he fell in that deep sleep approaching coma, the sleep made of pain and exhaustion, the sleep that was the body's own hiding place.

When he woke, the day had almost gone around, the soft violet of approaching dusk spreading through the trees. He let his eyes stare at the trees for a long moment, his body talk to him. The salve had worked wonders. His shoulder hurt, throbbed fiercely, but the intense, consuming pain was gone. With the arrowhead no longer pressing a nerve, the trembling and weakness had vanished. He pushed himself up on one elbow, winced, but stayed there. And he saw Jennifer and Clare appear.

Jennifer's eyes searched his face. "You look better," she observed.

"Feel better," he said.

She saw his eyes go to the trees behind her. "They'll be coming after us?" she asked.

He nodded slowly. "They have to. It's their way. Matter of saving face to themselves."

"When do you expect they'll get here?" she questioned.

"Morning, I'd guess," Fargo said. "By the time they corral those ponies, come back, and pick up my trail, it'll be dusk. They'll wait till morning to come after us."

"You won't be ready to ride in the morning," Clare said.

"No, I won't be," he agreed.

"I'm not leaving you," she said.

Jennifer spun on her. "You saying I'd leave him?" she snapped.

Clare shrugged. "I'm just saying I won't," she returned, not denying the unsaid.

"Stop sniping and start digging," Fargo cut in.

"Digging?" Clare frowned, Jennifer's face echoing the question.

"Got a plan. Only thing that might work," Fargo said, put his head back, rested some, then spoke to the two young women again. When he'd finished, he felt drained, but Clare and Jennifer helped him to his feet, half-carried him back into the trees, and lowered him onto a blanket there. He fell back. The short trip felt as though he'd just crossed country. The wound had begun to pain again and he was grateful for the exhaustion that sent him into a deep sleep. Night blanketed the forest and he continued to sleep, stayed asleep until the first gray of dawn drifted down through the spruce and balsam fir.

He opened his eyes, pulled himself up on his elbows, stretched one arm slowly. His extraordinary strength and recuperative powers had combined to let him feel better than most men would after a week's rest. The hole just below his shoulder, bandaged with torn strips of petticoat, stabbed pain at him, but it was pain he could stand. He peered through the trees. Jennifer and Clare had carried out his orders to perfection, he saw. The mound of earth rose from the forest floor, the crude cross fashioned of two branches at the head of it unmistakably marking it as a gravesite. Jennifer sat at one side of it, head bowed, hands clasped in her lap. Clare lay half across the mound of earth.

Fargo grunted in grim satisfaction, slowly turned himself around, fought away the pain, and took up the big Sharps Clare had put beside him as he'd asked. He lifted the rifle into his lap, curled his hand around the trigger, and rested his head back against a tree trunk. He dozed, let his ears read the tale of the forest life to him. He heard the flurried movement of ruffed grouse, the light steps of black-tailed deer. The odor of elk carried to him and the scurryings of snowshoe hare and weasel. But most of all, the air grew cold on his face, the harbinger he wanted least to meet.

He had come fully awake, but he rested with eyes closed when he caught the sound, the even-spaced touch of a horse moving through the forest. Two horses, he counted, and pulled his eyes open, his gaze riveted on the trees beyond the earthen mound. The two horsemen came into view, moving slowly, one with a long feather sticking up from his hair. Fargo watched the Arapaho see the gravesite, glance at each other, and move forward quickly. Clare and Jennifer heard them only when they were almost on them, stepping into the clearing from the trees. Clare stayed beside the mound and Jennifer leapt to her feet. The eagle feather moved his horse toward her, slowly, unhurried. He halted, looked down at the mound and then at Clare.

"Mountain man," he said, and Clare nodded.

The Arapaho leaned forward in the saddle and spit on the mound of earth. It was his last earthly gesture. Fargo, the big Sharps raised, fired and the Indian flew from his pony as if invisible wires had yanked him from the horse's back. Fargo fired again before the man hit the ground, the second Arapaho, trying to wheel his horse around, arched backward

106

as the bullet shattered the middle of his breastbone. He flung his arms into the air as he toppled to the ground, lay there unmoving except for the life's blood that ran from him, the dark-red stream carrying little pieces of bone along in it.

Fargo watched Jennifer and Clare gather their horses and his Ovaro, move to where he slumped down against the tree trunk. They lay down beside him and he closed his eyes, let sleep sweep over him again, the body making its own demands.

It was night when he woke. A tiny fire burned, just enough to heat a tin of soup. He sipped some Clare brought to him.

"I'll ride come morning," he said. Clare looked skeptical, snuggled down beside him, and Jennifer settled under the blanket she put down a few feet away. He was asleep again by the time the tiny fire burned out. When morning came, he woke, washed carefully, got his shirt on by himself. He stood up and tested legs. They protested a little, but only a little. His shoulder hurt when he lifted his left arm, but that, too, was bearable now. Clare was somewhere in the trees washing and he caught Jennifer's glance.

"I thought you'd really left me to them," she said.

"I wanted you to think that, act it out," he said.

"I'm sorry," she said. "I misjudged you."

"Thank Clare yet?" he asked. "She came along, put her neck on the line, too."

Jennifer's violet eyes hardened at once. "Not for me," she snapped. "Whatever she did, she did for you, to help keep you in one piece."

Acuity and accuracy, Fargo muttered to himself, they all had it to spare. "You still got the benefit of it," he said.

Jennifer's eyes didn't soften. "And I still want her on her way," she said.

He didn't answer, walked to the Ovaro, and carefully pulled himself into the saddle. It hurt, but it was bearable and he sat straight, drew his breath in as Clare returned, her jet hair no longer in braids but hanging loosely again, full and glistening.

"Let's move," he said, and turned the Ovaro northward. He rode slowly, had to rest often, and grimaced as they reached the end of the gentle hills and the pine forests and the mountains rose up sharply again. He kept a firm grip on the saddle horn with one hand as he sent the Ovaro climbing up a passageway. The towering peaks seemed to beckon with malevolent glee, opening up scars of little trails running upward as if in sadistic invitation. He followed one, then another, choosing the least steep ones that kept them moving northward. When the night came, he found a level place to rest; he slumped from the Ovaro and lay down in his bedroll, too tired to do more than nibble on a piece of beef jerky and fall into a deep sleep. He woke once during the night to feel his face chilled and he hunkered down deeper into the bedroll.

Morning came and he woke with replenished strength, more of it than he'd expected. He lay still and heard Jennifer's voice first, then Clare's, breaking in, angry exchanges. But cold fire this time, stubborn, acid exchanges.

"Fool, you're just a little fool," he heard Jennifer spit out.

"No, I'm not a fool," Clare returned.

Jennifer's voice took on snide superiority. "You really think he'd let you stay with him when this is over? God, what a fool," she said.

"Why wouldn't he?" Clare returned.

"He's not the kind. He's just using you, enjoying you, nothing else," Jennifer said venomously.

"You're just jealous, that's all," Clare said.

"No, but I'm paying him and you're in the way. He was almost killed because of you. He could've gotten away on the Ovaro with me, but he had to hang back and see that you were all right," Jennifer tossed out with ice and disdain.

"You're rotten," Clare hissed. "You'd say anything to make me leave. Well, I'm not leaving."

Jennifer's tone held acid. "You're wasting your time. You won't get him," she said.

"Neither will you," Clare said, and Fargo felt surprise at the deadliness in her voice. He heard someone turn, the rustle of clothing, and their voices grew still, an angry silence left simmering in the air. He pulled himself from his bedroll, still thinking about the angry exchange he had just heard. More than jealousy and bitchiness, he pondered, deep needs that collided, came out of different places, and he felt a strange foreboding run through him. But thoughts about the two young women swirled away on a gust of sharp wind as he dressed and saw the morning sky was a gray shroud. He peered up, seeking a break in the clouds that would offer optimism, but the grayness stayed solid and he led the Ovaro to where Jennifer and Clare were saddling their horses. Jennifer saw the grimness in his face at once, tossed a glance at the sky.

"Doesn't feel like snow to me," she said.

"Good," he snapped. "Because it sure as hell looks like it to me."

She mounted the dark-brown mare and followed him as he began to climb again. Clare swung in behind her, he saw, and the grimness stayed with him as the sky remained leaden. They rested often, and during one of the breaks he brought down a varying hare, its coat already more than half white. The thought of fresh meat for the night meal made him feel less uneasy, a good omen perhaps, he grunted. He moved on, led the way up through the afternoon, followed paths that led back and forth across the mountains, and tried to stay away from the punishing direct climbs.

But the air took on an added chill and the grayness overhead remained unbroken. They were on a cut through the face of a long slope, tamaracks at one side, a path that curved upward, when he heard the sound and he halted. Jennifer and Clare picked it up moments later, frowned at him. He pushed forward, up the passageway, and the sound grew louder, became sharp, a wavering, undulating sound, as if a thousand women were crying somewhere. He spurred the pinto on, hurried the horse around the slow curve, and the crying sound continued to grow louder. He pushed around the far end of the curve and the rocks came into view on a small table of land directly ahead, a dozen tall, basalt stones, each cut through with a least a half-dozen holes worn smooth, the result of ages of erosion and weather. The twelve smooth stones were facing one another in an irregular pattern so that the wind rushed through the holes from one to the other and back again to create the sound.

"Place of the Singing Rocks," he murmured, the Indian name more accurate as well as more beautiful.

Clare stared at the stones, her face still, hushed. "I remember, now," she breathed, "all the things I used to hear about this place. The singing rocks sing many songs. Every day it is different."

"Obviously it depends on the winds that blow through them," Jennifer commented crisply.

Clare's face remained hushed as she spoke. "The Indians believe the singing rocks are the voices of the spirit gods. They sing one way when they are pleased, another when they are angry."

Fargo saw Jennifer fix her with an arrogant stare. "I think you actually believe in that nonsense," Jennifer snapped.

Clare's eyes were veiled as they turned on her. "I believe in nothing and everything," she said softly.

"The spirit gods seem to be crying," Fargo said.

Clare nodded. "For something, someone," she murmured. "Let's go on, away from here."

Fargo glanced at the gray sky. It would make dusk come in earlier. Another hour's riding time, he figured, and saw Clare pull the map from her leather pouch. "It says north from the rocks," she told him, and he nodded, steered the Ovaro past the wild, wailing sounds that whistled through the rocks, moved north up the mountainside. He found a place to bed down as the night came. Jennifer passed him with her blankets on her way to the very edge of the campsite.

"I'm sure your little spirit maiden will want comforting," she remarked waspishly. "I'd rather not listen in."

"That much bitchiness must come natural," Fargo said.

Jennifer's violet eyes stayed unchanged. "And I want her gone before we reach that next cabin," she said.

"I'm not turning her loose alone up here," Fargo said.

"I've been telling you to turn her out all along. When we reach that cabin, I want all your attention on getting Slattery, not worrying about her little ass," Jennifer shot back, spun on her heel, and stalked away from him. She returned only when the hare was ready to eat, sat in silence with Clare across from her. Finished, she strode back to her blanket. Fargo smothered the fire, tossed the remains of the roasted hare over the side of the slope, and retired to his bedroll. The night grew inky black, with neither moon nor stars to pierce the total darkness. He lay in the bedroll, enveloped by the blackness, and felt the sharp wind dance over his face. The world became a stygian void and only the distant howl of a wolf reminded him that he was not suspended in some timeless state. Another sound finally came to break into the black void, tentative, groping footsteps.

"Over here," he whispered, and heard the steps change direction, a formless shape emerge out of the blackness. He spoke again and Clare half-stumbled over his bedroll, slipped to her knees, and he gathered her inside with him. She heard him wince as he half-turned toward her.

"No," she whispered. "Your shoulder needs a few days more. Just lie still with me, Fargo."

He lay back and she came half over him, pressed her breasts on his chest, the firm, large nipples soft little darts against his flesh. She lay quietly with him, unmoving, and he had decided she'd gone to sleep when he felt her fingers starting to trace a path along his stomach, down over his belly, move in a circle around his pelvis, slowly push through the thick denseness of his hair. He felt himself rising to welcome her, and when her fingers closed around him, he was pulsing, gathering strength. "Thought you said I was to lie still," he asked.

"Didn't say I would," she breathed, and he felt her hands, rubbing, stroking, fingers touching, exploring, curling around him, moving down across the loose skin beneath, cupping him in her grip. He felt her lips press down against his nipples, move down across his chest, little murmured sounds as she traced an oath with her lips. He felt the serpentine turning of her body as she came half over him, her lips moving along the side of his inner thigh, doubling back to move to his pelvis. He felt her legs moving, rubbing against him as her lips found him, opened wider, closed around him, warm, wet, her tongue a circling, darting soft column of fire. The soft half-moan, half-song came to him from inside his bedroll, broke off when she closed her mouth over him and he felt her shudder in ecstasy.

She made love to him, prolonged his explosion of desire, soothed even as she aroused, drank in all the turbulent sensations of desire and finally erupted herself, pushed her flowing warmth onto him, her face dug into his abdomen, her cry pressed into his flesh. He lay back, his strength not complete yet,

112

and felt turned inside out, drained, satisfied, and wanting only sleep. He was aware of her curled up beside him as he fell into a deep slumber, lay still in the total embrace of exhaustion, and was vaguely aware that he was alone when he turned on his side as the dawn neared.

When he woke, blinked, stared up at the sky, he swore softly. No dawn warmth, no bright sun to set the day afire, only the grayness again, filling every corner of the sky as far as the eye could see. He pushed himself from the bedroll, had washed and pulled on clothes before the two blankets stirred, came alive.

"Get yourselves together," he said. "I'll be back." He saw Clare sit up, eyes wide as he swung onto the Ovaro and rode away, but back the way they had come. He rode slowly, his eyes scanning the ground, taking in the hoofprints they had left as they'd climbed upward. The earth had hardened enough, surface frost casting the prints solidly in place. They'd stay that way, the earth past softening till the spring rains. Only a heavy snowfall would cover them.

He made an unhappy sound and turned the Ovaro when he found a place to do so, and he rode back to where Jennifer and Clare were dressed and waiting.

Jennifer's frown followed him to a halt. "What was that all about?" she questioned.

"Wanted to see what kind of a trail we were leaving," he said. "Too damn good a one."

She frowned. "You still think this man Davis is following?" she asked.

"That was his plan, it seemed. He was damn anxious. Can't see why he wouldn't keep on with it," Fargo said. He made his glance bland as he voiced the question. "Can you?" he asked.

"I told you, I don't know anything about him," Jennifer flared.

"So you did," Fargo agreed.

"Can we get moving?" she said testily. "You did have a good night's sleep, didn't you?"

"Damn good," he said, and moved the Ovaro forward. Jennifer and Clare mounted up, fell in close behind him. When he halted for a rest break in midmorning, Jennifer paused beside him.

"We could reach that cabin anytime," she said. He nodded agreement. "And she's still here," Jennifer hissed.

"Right again," he said.

"I told you I don't want you thinking about her when we reach it," Jennifer said, her voice an angry whisper.

"I'll do my job when the time comes, honey," he growled.

"I intend to be sure of that," Jennifer snapped, whirled on her heel, and climbed onto the brown mare. She sat simmering in the saddle and he had to admire the fiery, headstrong beauty of her. It could almost make him forget her selfish stubbornness. Almost.

He swung onto the Ovaro and rode on, and it was when he halted again in the afternoon that Clare came up along side him and he saw the held-in fury in her angular face. "I heard her back there," Clare muttered. "Bitch. All she cares about is herself. I hope she never finds Slattery."

"Might turn out that way," Fargo said as his eyes went to the gray sky. "You stay cool. Nothing's going to be better by spitting at each other." Clare's silence seemed agreement, but the dark fury in her face told him otherwise. He quickened the pace as the passage stayed gentle, and he was beginning to think the day would pass quietly when he felt the soft wetness against his face. He glanced up, saw the white flecks become a thin veil of flakes before his eyes. The snowfall continued to gather strength, but it came down softly, no wind driving it, quickly laying a thin blanket of white over the slopes. Another time and another place he might have enjoyed the soft snowfall, but here he saw only the harbinger of white fury. Clare's words echoed his fears.

"The mountains talk," she said. "They warn. They send their messages."

Jennifer's voice, instant anger, cut in. "The message is turn back? Oh, you'd like that, wouldn't you?" she said. "Well, I'm prepared for a little snow."

Clare shrugged and Fargo moved his horse on, his eyes peering through the light veil of falling snow. The passage they rode began to narrow, and his gaze lifted to the towering crag that rose up directly ahead of them. He continued on as the pathway narrowed further. The huge, craggy peak grew wider and higher as he neared it, mostly rock with hardy mountain brush and a handful of windswept balsams high up near the top. He had almost reached it when the Ovaro suddenly leapt into the air, both forefeet striking up and out, and Fargo felt himself go backward, clutched at the saddle horn, and stopped himself from being thrown. The Ovaro's feet came down, but the horse held his right foreleg up and Fargo saw the length of wood sticking from the horse's hoof.

"Damn," he swore as he leapt to the ground, took hold of the Ovaro's leg, and examined the length of wood, saw that one end, sharp as a lance, had gone deep into the soft, tender frog of the hoof. He yanked the length of branch out with one quick motion and peered at the deep cut in the frog. He let the Ovaro's leg go and the horse put it on the ground, held it up at once.

Jennifer and Clare halted beside him and he kicked the length of branch. "Never saw it there. The snow had it half-covered," he said as he took the jar of salve from his saddlebag and applied the ointment into the frog. "Easy, now," he murmured soothingly as the horse tried to pull away. Satisfied he'd put enough into the wound, he let the leg go and saw the Ovaro hold it gingerly, not placing any weight on it.

"I'll walk him," he said, and led the Ovaro forward by the cheek strap. The horse limped behind him for the dozen yards before he halted, the towering crag blocking the path. He dropped the reins and stepped closer to the huge peak, saw Jennifer and Clare come after him.

He was frowning as he peered at the path that led up one side of the mountain, a curving, narrow ledge of dirt and stone, barely large enough for one horse at a time to fit. It curved, followed the outside of the crag, disappeared from sight as it continued up against the mountain. Fargo's glance moved back and forth across the towering crag as the snow lessened, came to a halt suddenly. He saw Jennifer's eyes stare at the narrow ledge that was the sole pathway up the mountainside. He answered the thought that gathered in her eyes. "There's no other way," he said. "Not on this side of that crag." He scanned the gray sky that seemed low enough to almost touch. "We'll look at it, come morning. It'll be dark in half an hour," he said. He saw a rock overhang at the base of the huge crag and moved toward it, the Ovaro limping after him. The overhang provided a rock roof over the small area, more than enough to buffer the sharp wind that whistled down the sides of the crag.

He watched Clare and Jennifer bring their horses under the overhang, position them next to the Ovaro.

"Doesn't leave much room," Clare said.

"No, we'll bed down in close quarters tonight. We'll need all the rest we can get for tomorrow," he said.

Clare's eyes, as she threw him a quick glance, revealed that she got the message.

The night came quickly; they ate hardtack and he laid out his bedroll, crawled into it. Jennifer put her blanket beside him and Clare bedded down at the other side of her. He slept quickly, refused to let himself think about the seemingly impossible passageway that waited a half-dozen yards away. Morning would be time enough for that.

The night wind had blown a good part of the light snowfall away when morning came, but Fargo, standing away from the rock overhang, saw that the narrow pathway along the side of the crag looked even less possible to climb. He walked to where it began along the lower base of the craggy peak, saw the sheer drop over the one side and the rock cliff of the crag on the other. He peered up along the ledge until it curved out of sight up the peak, and he turned, walked to the Ovaro, and swung into the saddle. He let the horse take a half-dozen steps, more than enough to show that the horse still limped, his steps tentative. Fargo demanded a sudden leap forward and the Ovaro responded but threw his hindquarters sideways as pain shot up his foreleg. Fargo pulled him to a halt, bounded to the ground, and saw Jennifer and Clare watching him.

"No good," he muttered. "Not for what we'll need."

"What's that?" Jennifer asked.

"A horse to go up ahead of the rest of us, test out the ledge, see if it'll hold. That means a horse able to react quick, move straight, jump fast if he has to— the Ovaro, if he was himself."

"Use my horse," Jennifer said.

"Suicide. He doesn't have the legs, the strength, or the reaction time for what he'll need," Fargo said.

"My gray does," Clare said.

Fargo thought for a moment, his gaze going to the gray gelding, the short, powerful legs, the strong hindquarters, no distance speed in him but more than enough for close-quarter work. "Maybe," Fargo said slowly. "I could try."

He saw Clare shake her head. "Not you. Me," she

said. "He won't take a strange rider, not on a place like that."

Fargo's eyes peered hard at her. "Could be your last ride," he said.

"Yours for sure, if you try to take him up there," she said, shrugging.

His lips thinned grimly and he cast an eye at the sky, low-hanging cirrus clouds gathering again in the distance. The Ovaro wouldn't be ready to ride lead on that ledge for another three days, and this was no place to be caught if the snows came heavy. He had no choice and he cast a glance at Jennifer. She had set a mask over her face, waited without expression.

He shrugged helplessly. "No choice, is there?" he said, and Clare nodded back agreement.

"The gray and I can do it," she said.

He beckoned to her and she walked the half-dozen yards to the base of the peak where the narrow ledge began its steep, circling climb. "You start five minutes ahead of us. Take it very slow, test every step," he told her. "God knows what you'll find. It might get better. It might get worse." His mouth tightened. "I'd guess worse," he said. "You get in trouble, stay there till I reach you." He paused, took his eyes from the crag to search her face. "You have butterflies inside, then don't do it," he warned. "You know your horse will pick it up from you."

"No butterflies." She half-smiled. "I just want to get all this over with, get rid of that bitch so we can be by ourselves."

He nodded, turned, started back to the overhang. Once again, she was acting for herself. Jennifer would gain by it without the need to feel any gratitude. Wasn't right, somehow, he mused silently.

Clare climbed onto her horse as Jennifer watched from a distance.

Fargo stepped back. "Remember, slow and easy," he said.

Clare nodded as she sent the gray gelding forward, the horse starting up the narrow ledge with smooth, easy strides.

Fargo moved to one side, watched Clare go up, staying close to the side of the crag. He watched her till she disappeared from sight as the narrow path curved up around the crag. He strode to the Ovaro, mounted, and looked across at Jennifer. "Let's move," he said, felt the furrow form on his brow as Jennifer stared up at the ledge as if transfixed. "Time to move," he said again, louder, and saw Jennifer wrench her eyes from the ledge with an effort, stare at him. "What's the matter?" He frowned.

Her eyes darkened with a strange turbulence. She looked away, turned, and pulled herself on her horse.

"Just stay behind me. Take it slow. Call out if you're having trouble," he told her as he moved to the base of the ledge. He glanced at her. She stared downward, her face tight, and he saw her lick her lips nervously. Fear, he guessed, a sudden attack of raw fear. He'd seen it happen to others, always unexpected, always sudden.

He started up the narrow ledge, turned his concentration on the task ahead. The Ovaro's limp made him nervous and he knew it made the horse nervous, too, unsure of himself, edgy because of it. He stroked the warm, beautiful neck, soothed the horse. He glanced back at Jennifer and her eyes met his for an instant, staring, almost distraught. Fear, he said again to himself, and yet something more than fear, a strange inner turmoil.

He turned back to moving his own horse carefully along the ledge. It rose sharply, stayed dangerously narrow. He felt the Ovaro's limp growing worse and he sat back in the saddle to help balance the upward pull. His glance went down the sheer drop at the other side of the ledge and he saw jagged clusters of rock jutting out from the side of the cliff as if waiting to finish anything that survived the fall.

He looked behind again, frowned as he watched Jennifer ride, her face still rigid, eyes held downward. "You all right?" he called, and she glanced up at him and the same, strange turmoil lay in the violet eyes. " Stay close to the wall," he said.

She looked away from him, not answering, and he turned back to making his own way. But he felt the frown stay on his brow. Not just fear, he decided, corrected his first guess. Something else inside her, something the danger and tension had made surface. He called back, put soothing reassurance in his voice. "We'll make it. Just take it nice and easy. You'll be fine," he said.

She didn't answer and he glanced back. Her lovely lips were thinned into a narrow line and her eyes stayed downcast again. He grunted, returned his attention to the Ovaro. The horse's limp continued to grow worse and he could feel the animal's nervous hesitation increasing. He found a spot where the narrow ledge allowed a few inches more, and he slid from the saddle, scrambled up to the horse's head, felt his foot go over the edge and gasped, caught hold of the saddle, and hung on. The Ovaro moved forward and he felt himself pulled up and forward, got one foot dug in, regained balance. He halted the horse, leaned against the powerful shoulders, and let his breath return.

He glanced back. Jennifer was staring, her mouth open. "It's all right," he said. "My fault. Got careless. Keep coming. I'm going to walk the Ovaro," Fargo said. Her eyes continued to stare at him, as if he had said nothing, consumed in some private terror. He took the Ovaro's reins and started up the path again, pausing only to wipe the film of perspiration that had coated his face despite the sharp, cold wind. The narrow ledge curved, hugged the side of the crag, continued to stay frighteningly narrow. It curved upward as the peak rose in a seemingly unending spiral. The pinto's limp was better without a rider on his back and Fargo used the reins much as he would, had he been in the saddle, guiding, pulling back, steering the horse in close to the wall when the ledge grew narrower.

Clare was too far ahead by now to even glimpse as the ledge climbed in a circle against the peak. The ledge suddenly made a dip and a sharp turn against the rock side of the crag as the wall recessed unexpectedly. Fargo had to push back quickly with the reins, grab the Ovaro by the noseband, and edge the horse around the sharp recess. He halted where the ledge straightened, watched Jennifer guide the brown mare slowly around the spot, her face made of tension, her hands gripping the reins so hard that they were drained of blood. Again, he tried to soothe her, kept his voice low, calm. "You're doing fine . . . just fine . . . that's it, now . . . that's it," he said as she brought the horse past the critical point. She halted as she reached the straight portion of the ledge, and he nodded reassuringly at her. "Let's keep moving," he said. "We'll make it."

"You see her?" Jennifer breathed.

"Clare? No, she's too far ahead to see with the way the ledge curves along the mountain," he answered. "Not seeing her's a good sign. Means she's making it, the ledge passable."

"No," Jennifer said, and the single word seemed to tear from her throat. "She's going to fall," Jennifer said. "I know it."

"Easy, now," Fargo said calmly. "This is no time to get wild ideas. Just take it easy."

"No wild ideas," Jennifer said, and the wild turmoil was stark in her eyes, which stared at him. "She's going to fall. I know it," she repeated. He saw veins suddenly standing out in her long, lovely neck. He started to try to calm her again, but she tore words out again. "I loosened the cinch on her saddle," she blurted out.

Fargo heard the words, but it took a long moment

for the impact to strike at him. He felt disbelief, shock, time suddenly coming to a halt. "You what?" He frowned, not certain he was hearing things right.

"I loosened the cinch," Jennifer cried out. "When you and she were talking. Oh, God, I did it and I want to take it back. I want to take it back and I can't."

Fargo felt the disbelief and shock explode in rage, but a rage compounded by a rush of fear and helplessness. "You bitch," he shouted. "You stinking, rotten little murderin' bitch." He wanted her to see the rage inside him, but Jennifer had her eyes closed, her face lifted upward, and her words were a wild and wailing sound.

"Oh, God, oh, God, oh God . . ." She cried out. "Oh, God."

"Goddamn," Fargo shouted, tossed the Ovaro's reins over the horse's neck, and started to run, racing up the narrow ledge with all the power desperation and fury could give. He dug heels into the ledge, felt his left foot go out from under him as the edge of dirt crumbled. He dived forward, rolled against the opposte wall, and heard the sound of dirt and stones crashing down to the jagged rocks below. Pulling himself to his feet, he raced on, around the curving ledge. "Damn," he swore into the wind as he ran. "Goddamn bitch. Crazy goddamn bitch." The curses filled the cold air as he rounded a curved place and tried to fight away the feeling of helplessness. He peered up the ledge and swore again as she was still out of sight

He ran, slipped, stumbled, kept running—recklessly, he knew—yet speed, not caution, pushed him forward. The ledge curved again and he raced around it, his eyes widening as he saw her, the gray gelding at the top of another curve. He started to call out and the words froze in his throat as he saw the horse's hind legs slip, go off the edge. He saw Clare's slender form slide from the horse, curiously

122

slow as she fell through the air. The horse followed, did a back flip, the large gray shape turning as it fell.

"Goddamn . . . Jesus, oh, goddamn," Fargo swore, fell to one knee. He pounded the narrow ledge with his fists in total, helpless frustration. "Too late, a half-minute too goddamn late," he swore. He rose, ran on to where she and the gray had gone over. A line of rocks protruded from the otherwise sheer side, Clare's form lying on them, twisted, the horse nearby, its neck turned half around.

Fargo swung himself over the edge of the narrow path, the slope inclined enough to slide down, a cover of scrub brush clinging to it. He let himself go, felt his body pick up instant momentum as he slid. He reached out, grasped hold of brush, slowed his slide. He felt the loose dirt and stones going with him, raining down on him, and he saw the rocks coming up fast. He drew his legs up, landed on the balls of his feet, rolled, hit against one jagged piece with his side, and gasped in pain. He halted on his hands and knees, Clare but a few yards from him. He crawled over the rocks to her, cursing as he did, reached her side. Except for the twisted position of her torso and the slow dark-rust stain seeping through her clothes, she seemed asleep, her face unmarked.

He reached out, touched her cheek, and her eyelids fluttered, came open. "Christ," Fargo said. "Jesus, honey, I'm sorry; good God, I'm sorry."

Her lips moved, words following slowly, barely audible. "One mistake," she said. "One lousy mistake."

He shook his head and felt the rage flame up inside him. "No mistake. She did it," he said. "She loosened the cinch on you. Goddamn bitch did it. She'll pay, goddammit, she'll pay."

Clare's eyes stared at him, taking in his words. "For me," she breathed. "For me."

He nodded, his jaw throbbing with fury. "She'll

pay, for you, goddamn her stinkin' hide. She'll pay," he promised. He saw the tiny smile come, touch her lips for an instant, a fleeting moment of satisfaction, and then her eyes closed and a final, quick shudder shook her body and she lay still.

"Goddamn," Fargo whispered, stayed for a moment more, and then rose; in his eyes there was a consuming rage.

He made his way across the jagged rocks, flung a quick glance at the lifeless form of the horse as he passed, rage at Jennifer consuming his thoughts. Rage and a kind of horrible awe at the depths selfishness and jealousy could reach. She'd pay, he muttered, and felt his fingers twitch with the urge to strangle her. She had gotten a last-minute attack of conscience, but that didn't change the monstrousness of it. That was too little and too late. She had told him she intended to be sure he wouldn't have Clare to think about when they found Slattery. She'd told him, and he hadn't realized, hadn't understood, and the awesomeness of it still defied understanding.

He reached the steep side, grasped one of the dry mountain brush that clung to the slope. He started to pull himself up, suddenly stopped, and let himself slide back. The frown dug into his forehead and he suddenly felt as if he'd been struck in the pit of the stomach. "No, dammit," he muttered as he turned. He started back across the jagged rocks, hurrying, another kind of unbelief flooding over him. He had to be sure. The mind played tricks, especially when overheated. He reached the still form of the horse and stared down at it, felt his mouth drop open. He stared for a long minute. The saddle was in place on the lifeless form. Even after the fall, the saddle was still in place, the cinch holding tight.

"Aw, Jesus," Fargo breathed as he dropped to one knee, astonishment, awe, a kind of incomprehension, all whirling inside him. He forced his mind to stop spinning, put thoughts in order, piece the facts in front of him together.

Jennifer had loosened the cinch. There was no question on that. It had been there in her eyes, the stark horror of her own act. He had seen it as fear when it was guilt. But the cinch was tight around the lifeless horse, which meant only one thing: Clare had discovered it loose, stopped, and tightened it. She had fallen because she'd made a mistake—her words, which he'd brushed aside, but they'd been true. The saddle hadn't slipped. She'd simply fallen.

He heard the deep breath of air rush from him. The other part of it curled in the pit of his stomach, stayed there like some undigestible bone. But he had to digest it, face it. Clare had known, of course, and with her dying words, had been willing to let him vent all his rage at Jennifer. That tiny little smile of satisfaction had been exactly that—the last laugh, a final victory. He turned away and felt strangely shaken, as though he had witnessed forces beyond his understanding. The female of the species is deadlier than the male. Someone had told him that once. He knew the truth of it in other creatures. It was no less true with his own kind, he had learned.

He began to pull himself up the steep side, the climb long, slow, and hard on muscle and flesh. He reached the top finally, pulled himself onto the narrow ledge, and lay unmoving until his breath returned and his arms stopped aching. He rose and went back down the ledge to where the Ovaro had halted, Jennifer on her horse close behind him. He saw the horror in her eyes, a staring emptiness that was nonetheless filled with pain.

"Follow me," he said gruffly. "I'll talk to you when we get off this damn ledge."

He took the reins and moved the Ovaro forward, reached the place where Clare had gone over, kept the horse close to the other edge, saw that Jennifer did the same. The ledge stayed as narrow, every step fraught with danger, death waiting for another mistake. Jennifer seemed drained, no longer consumed with guilt, emptied of all feeling. But with the searing tension out of her, the brown mare calmed, moved more securely behind the Ovaro, and it was with relief that Fargo saw the ledge come to an end, broaden out onto a stand of high timber, tamaracks mostly, and he reached the top, pulled the Ovaro to one side, and helped draw the mare up.

Jennifer slid from the saddle and sank down on the ground, her eyes dulled with pain as he came over to her. "You didn't do it," he said.

Jennifer stared at him, uncomprehending.

"Clare fell, got too close to the edge, and went over. It wasn't your fault," he said.

She shook her head, rejected his words. "I loosened the cinch, that's why she fell," Jennifer murmured, and put her face into her hands.

"The cinch was tight. The saddle was in place," he said.

Slowly, as if sleepwalking, she lifted her face from her hands, stared up at him.

"I saw it," he said. "She stopped somewhere along the way and tightened it."

Jennifer's eyes were round saucers as she stared at him. "Oh, my God," she breathed. "Oh, thank God. Oh, Jesus." She continued to stare up at him as she drew in deep breaths of the cold air, the tan buckskin jacket moving up and down with each deep draft. "Thank you for telling me," she said gratefully. "You could have held back."

"Thought about it," he said. "Let you stew in your own guilt some more. You deserve that."

She looked down at her hands in her lap. "Yes, I suppose so," she murmured. "But I did tell you," she said. "I couldn't go through with it."

"That supposed to make everything all right?" he shot back. "It might've been too late by the time you told me."

126

Jennifer looked away, his words striking hard. "No, it doesn't make everything all right," she said. "I guess I'm trying to live with myself."

"That'll take some doing," he growled. "Mount up. We've most of the afternoon left."

He swung onto the Ovaro; on relatively level ground the horse limped less, and Fargo saw a wide swath through the tamaracks that led upward, fairly easy riding land, and he took it. He rested the Ovaro often, and the day started to close down, the wind growing colder.

Jennifer had followed in complete silence, stayed behind him, and came up alongside the Ovaro only when he halted, pointed through the tamaracks at the little log cabin. A tiny gasp of anticipation escaped her as she peered at the cabin. She started forward and he pulled her back. He slid from the saddle, motioned to her, and she dismounted.

"It's waiting time," he said.

6

"Dammit, he's not in there," Jennifer hissed. "We've been out here watching the place for almost two hours."

"He could be asleep inside," Fargo said calmly. "Or he could be out hunting dinner and be on his way back. Either way you could get your head blown away."

"How long do we wait here? I'm freezing," she said.

He shifted position behind the tamarack, watched dusk sliding over the mountain peaks. "Another half-hour. It'll be dark then. He'll be coming back by then, if he's anywhere near; and if he's asleep inside, we can get close without getting our tails shot off," he told her. She settled down again, unhappily, and Fargo scanned the little cabin again. A solid, well-built cabin, a short stone chimney jutting above the log roof at one end. A mountain man had built it at one time, made it strong enough to stand the screaming winters. He saw a covered area attached to the back for keeping the horses. The cabin beckoned invitingly, but he hadn't come this far to grow careless, and he let the night follow the gray-purple of dusk. The cabin stayed dark and Fargo rose to his feet, unholstered the big Colt .45, and started forward.

"Leave the horses. I'll come back for them," he said as he moved in a crouch. A handful of trees had been chopped down to make a clear space outside the cabin, the stumps still in place, and he crossed the clearing in quick, long strides.

Jennifer stayed close behind him, he saw as he reached the cabin, pressed himself against the outside wall, and listened. He heard nothing and he moved to the door, motioned for her to stay back. He crossed to the other side of the wood door and lifted his leg, kicked hard, and the door flew open as he jumped back. But no flurry of bullets exploded from inside the cabin and he slid around the edge of the door, crouched, the Colt ready to fire. He felt his breath push from him as he straightened.

"Empty," he called, and Jennifer came as he stepped inside. He saw a small railroad man's lamp hanging on one wall, found ample fluid in it, and got it lighted. It flooded the single room with more-than-enough light.

Fargo saw a wood cot against one wall, a three-legged table, and a handmade stool whittled out of pine. A dozen pieces of split wood were in a stack near the fireplace and a long-handled ax rested against the stones of the chimney. Dust had been cleared away from the table area, and Jennifer, rummaging through the cabin, came up with another piece of the green-dyed tobacco pouch paper.

"He was here," she said, frowned in consternation. "Dammit, where'd he go?"

"The map say anything more?" Fargo asked.

She fished it from her pouch at once, shook her head as she looked at it. "No, cabin is the last mark on it. This is it," she said. "Maybe he's just out someplace and he's coming back."

"No," Fargo said. "Man figuring to come back doesn't take everything with him. He's cleared out." Fargo scanned the little signs, the inside of the fireplace, the areas cleared of dust still clean. "He hasn't been gone long. Maybe a day or two," he said.

"We didn't meet him on the way up here. He

must've gone down the other side of the mountain,'' Jennifer said.

"Might get a line on that, come daylight,'' Fargo said. "I'll get the horses. You start a fire,'' he said as the cold wind penetrated into the cabin. He left and walked back to the horses as he felt the thought pushing at him. Somethind didn't set right. Slattery had plainly followed his plan, and yet it seemed he'd come an awful hard and long way, far into the high mountain country, just to hide out a spell. Maybe he intended it to be different, Fargo pondered as he started back with the horses. Maybe he intended to hole up for the winter but saw that he hadn't time to prepare. Logical thoughts, but they failed to satisfy, and he put further speculation aside as he sniffed the night air. He swore inwardly as he drew in the damp cold of it, the feel of snow hanging close. He unsaddled the horses, secured them under the overhang behind the cabin, and went back inside, where Jennifer had a fire blazing, had some jerky warming in a skillet and an old white coffeepot on.

"I turned the lamp out. There's not much oil left in it,'' she said.

He sat down before the fire and she settled beside him as he ate in silence. She waited till he'd finished, sipped the coffee she poured into tin mugs that were in the cabin. "You thinking about Clare?'' she asked quietly.

"Trying not to,'' he said. "Don't see much gain in it. There'll be time enough to think about her when this is done with.'' He peered at her as she stared into the fire. "You?'' he asked.

She shook her head and little shafts of orange-red seemed to shoot out into the air as the firelight danced over her. "Thinking about Slattery,'' she said. "You pick up his tracks, come morning, and we go after him. I didn't come all this way to give up on finding him." She jumped in fright as a sudden hard gust of wind rattled the cabin door.

"We might not be going anywhere, come morning," Fargo said.

"Just the mountain winds," Jennifer answered. "You've been wrong so far."

"I haven't been wrong. You've been lucky," he said as he got to his feet. "Put a coat on. I saw a lot of deadwood all around here. I want it all inside here."

"We're going to fetch wood in the dark?" she said.

"Before we run out of time," he said. "Leave the cabin door open. That'll give us enough light to work with."

She rose, put the tan buckskin jacket on with obvious disdain. "I do think you tend to exaggerate things," she sniffed.

He paused, his eyes hardening on her. "And you tend to dumbness," he said. "There's no living man can exaggerate the Rocky Mountain winter storms when they come. Now move your ass and start bringing in every piece of wood you can carry."

He stalked out, left the cabin door hanging open, and began to gather the wood that lay all round the cabin. Some had been left by whoever built the cabin, old and dry, almost too dry to burn well, but there was plenty of good wood left by last winter's storms. He worked hard, carried armful after armful into the cabin, and Jennifer hauled her weight, finally protested when he had one wall stacked high. "God, don't you think we've enough?" she said.

"Yes, if we're lucky. No, if we're not," he said. "You keep hauling in more while I rig the tarpaulin up for the horses." He went outside to the rear of the cabin, hung the large tarp up on the north side of the overhang. It would keep the snow and wind from blowing directly on the animals, and there were enough oats on hand for the better part of a week if

131

the snows were too deep for them to get at the mountain grasses. He returned to the cabin and closed the door.

Jennifer had brought in enough for one more stack against the wall and she had taken her coat off, knelt before the fire.

"Let it burn down for the night and use your blanket," he said. Another hard gust of wind slammed against the door and he saw the moment of fright flash in her violet eyes. She recovered quickly, though, and her headstrong stubbornness was her reservoir of strength, he decided. Pretty much all surface, yet she wrapped it around her as a shield. He laid out his own bedroll, watched the fire burn down to embers, and rose and went to the door. There was no bolt on it and he pushed the chair against it. She was still beside the almost-out fire when he turned, started to undress, and smiled as she kept her back to him.

"Going to have to cut down on your modesty unless you figure to go outside and undress," he said. He glanced at his saddlebag and the big Sharps that he'd brought in. "I've no salve for frozen buns," he said.

Her back stayed to him and he undressed to his shorts, lay down on his bedroll when she got to her feet, turned to him, almost silhouetted against the dim glow of the remaining embers. He felt the surprise catch at him as she began to undress, facing him, slipping out of her shirt first, then undoing the skirt, dropping it to the floor. She wore almost-knee-length bloomers and the surprise had dug a frown into his brow as she stepped out of the last undergarment.

She came toward him, half-turned, and there was enough light for him to see the full ripeness of her; breasts very round, creamy, little nipples that lay flat against light-pink circles. He let his eyes go down a broad rib cage, womanly hips, and a little convex belly that curved down to a triangular nap that, even in the dimness, he saw was not dark. Full hips, but beautifully molded, curving into nice legs, thighs excitingly fleshy, a thoroughly sensual body, seen, as he did now, in all its nakedness, a body that echoed the fiery headstrongness of her.

The flesh follows the spirit, he murmured silently.

Jennifer sank down to her knees before him. "Surprised," she said. "You'd have to be."

"Surprised," he echoed.

"You've been driving me mad every night since she came with us," Jennifer said, and he heard the anger come into her voice. "Every goddamn night."

"You're full of surprises," Fargo said.

"To myself, too," she bit out. "I never felt that way before, not about anyone. Never knew I could. Or would," she added reflectively.

"Nothing like a bad case of jealousy to bring out what's inside," Fargo commented, his eyes moving over the full ripeness of her breasts.

"It's not that simple," Jennifer said. "I think it's being wound up tight inside and something with these mountains. They're raw, primitive. They tear civilization away from you and you don't know they're doing it."

"Maybe it was waiting to be torn away," he said.

She leaned to him. "Yes, maybe," she breathed, and he felt her breasts against his chest, downy soft. She leaned closer, pressed harder, the downy softness giving in, flattening against him. Her mouth came onto his—open, wet—and he felt her tongue moving out, circling, demanding. She pulled back a fraction. "All those nights, damn you, Fargo. Make me forget them," she breathed.

He kissed her, lips pressing her mouth open wider, and he sent his tongue darting into her warm softness, a messenger she welcomed. Jennifer's hands grasped his face, pulled him down to her full, creamy breasts, rubbed his mouth against them, sweet cushions enveloping his face. He caught hold of one flat little pink nipple as it passed across his face, bit gently yet hard enough to halt her. "Oh," she gasped, and he let his tongue circle the flat tip. He felt it rise, grow firmer, yet it stayed small and he touched the tiny protuberance with his teeth. She gasped and her hands moved hard into his shoulders.

He opened his mouth wider, sucked, pulled her breast in deep, caressed it with his tongue, pulled on it, painted it with his lips. "Jesus, oh, God, Fargo . . . Oh, Jesus," Jennifer cried out. He pulled back, pushed himself atop her for a moment, and let his warm, throbbing organ press into the little convex belly. Jennifer's arms wrapped themselves around his neck, and her lips murmured little sounds into the side of his face. He shifted, moved from atop her, and she cried out in protest but the cry was snapped off as his hand moved caressingly down her body, cupped her breasts, went down across the broad rib cage, pressed gently into her little belly, and rubbed through the soft-firm pubic hair, rested on the mound that curved upward against his palm.

Jennifer's full-fleshed thighs moved together, then came apart, and he felt her hands fluttering up and down his back, unable to find a place to hold, rest, and he let his hand drop to the dark opening and slip inside.

"Aaaah, ah, Christ, ah, you bastard, you bastard . . . take me, Fargo . . . Jesus, take me, I can't wait anymore, I can't wait." He heard the sob in her voice—desperation, pleading, and protest all mingled together. But he explored deeper with his fingers, stroked, felt the tightness of her, let his finger trace little circular motions inside her.

"Oh, ohh, oh . . . oh, God, oh, God," Jennifer gasped and he felt her hands become little fists, pound into his back. "Now, now, now, damn you," she screamed, but he held back, the sense of the sensual, the wisdom of the flesh. She was ready, yet unready, and he felt the edge of a special pleasure in bringing her wild wanting still higher.

He pressed deeper with his fingers, drew back, touched the quivering edges of the warm, wet lips, and she all but leapt from his arms, orange-red hair flying back and forth, sweeping against his face, exciting sensation of its own. A few strands caught in his mouth, and he felt himself being swept along with the totality of the raw desire Jennifer Carlyle flung forth, every touch, every sensation given new heights. He brought his hand from her, pressed it into the soft flesh of her inner thighs, pressed her legs wider apart, and saw her hips lift, begin to pump for him.

"Now, now, now, damn you, damn you," Jennifer screamed, her head tossing from side to side against the bedroll. But she could reach still higher, he sensed, and he pushed his face between her inner thighs and she brought her legs together against him as she screamed. "Aaaaah . . . aaaaaiiiii . . . Fargo . . . you . . . you . . . oh, God."

He pulled his face up, pulling away from the soft vise, and with his hands, pressed her thighs open again. She screamed in mounting fervor, her legs parted and waiting in a position that sent her into spiraling frenzy. As her body lifted, shook, and she screamed at him, he came over her, drove into her, and felt her tightness around him at once, wonderful capture, the bonds of ecstasy. He drove into her, drew back, and drove in again, thrustings that were welcomed by screams for more, and he heard a note of pain that was drowned out by pleasure. No sinuous writhings for Jennifer, a total, enveloping physical absorption, every part of her body responding, the flesh past control, mistress of body and soul. Suddenly her screams and cries halted and he felt her fingers dig into the back of his legs.

"Oh, no," Jennifer gasped, her voice hushed. "Oh, no." The strange instant of suspended motion hung on. "Oh, no . . . no . . . oh, no." Jennifer's gasped cries rose, grew stronger, and the moment shattered. Her fingers stayed dug into his legs and her ripe body rose upward, drew back, and slammed up against him. Her scream exploded with the suddenness of a cougar's wail, piercing, almost earsplitting, a shriek that held all the world's ecstasy inside it. The shriek filled the cabin, hung in the air, finally trailed away into little gasped sounds. "Jesus . . . oh, God almighty," Jennifer breathed as she lay with her abdomen sucking inward, pushing out, the body still responding to the senses.

She turned in his arms as he finally drew from her, and her lips found his mouth, soft, pliant lips. "Only once before, Fargo," she whispered, "when I was just a kid. Nothing, then, exploring, wondering, nothing more. But this was more than I expected. God, so much more. Maybe I've been waiting too long, holding back too long."

"Maybe," he said. "But I'm glad I was around when you decided to stop."

She lay back with him, took his hand, and cupped it under the soft fullness of one breast. "Me, too," she murmured, sighed, and he felt her relax against him, heard the shallow softness of her breathing as she went to sleep. He lay back and closed his eyes. Jennifer had done the unexpected from the very first moment she'd come into his life. He had the very distinct feeling she was not finished yet. He went to sleep with the hope that anything more would be as pleasurable as the last, wondered dimly why he was filled with misgivings on that.

The howling of the wind woke him as morning filtered into the cabin. Windowless, the cabin had a square of pine hinged on one side that could be pulled open to look out. He rose, left Jennifer covered inside the bedroll, and built a fire up. He went to the wood square, certain of what he'd find when he pulled it open. The blast of frigid air rushed in at him first, the swirl of driving snow charging after it. He peered outside, a driving curtain of snow all but obliterating his vision. No more gentle warnings now, the mountains roaring their fury, a howl of white, blanketing rage. He pushed the square of wood shut, latched it, and saw Jennifer's head lift as she came awake.

"You won't be finding any tracks this morning," he said. She lay back down and he passed her, took a large porcelain basin in one corner of the room, opened the cabin door, and scooped it full of snow. He brought it back to stand near the fire as he stayed to stop his own shivering. The snow melted quickly to become water for heating in the iron pot that was in the cabin. He dressed, went outside to where he'd spied a very crude outhouse, and returned half-frozen. When Jennifer made the trip, she came back and fell before the fire, curled herself like a cat until she thawed out. He made coffee, and when she took the tin cup from him, her violet eyes held defiance.

"I'm not giving up," she muttered.

"Might be you'll have to decide something else then," he said. "Whether you want to freeze to death or starve to death."

"I don't have to decide that yet," she said.

"No, not yet," he agreed. "But you keep thinking time stands still."

Her eyes softened suddenly and a little smile came to her lips. "It did last night," she said. She downed the coffee, turned to him. "Make it stand still again," she said, began to pull off clothes, and was beautifully naked before she reached his bedroll.

The little nap he'd only glimpsed in the darkness was a reddish hue, he saw now, a soft echo of the flame of her hair. She stretched out, sweet-violet eyes darkened, and watched as he shed clothes, came down beside her. The full ripeness of her seemed more so now, light a confirmation of beauty, her breasts beautifully rounded, their cream downiness an invitation to touch, caress, kiss. It was an invitation he happily accepted, and he heard the slow sigh of pleasure that escaped her lips as he took one lovely breast into his mouth, caressed the flat little point with his tongue. The howl of the storm outside faded away in the wildness of her gasping, crying wanting.

"Oh, Jesus, Fargo . . . oh, God, like last night, please, like last night," she pleaded as he set her body aflame with hands, fingers, lips. She demanded quickly again, the eager wanting a leaping, anxious, almost fearful urge, as though she were afraid the moment of climax would somehow slip away unfulfilled. But once again he held back, and her feverish wanting reached new heights, her full-fleshed legs pulling up and open for him, her pubic mound lifting in little eager spasms, the very act adding to her wanting.

"Please, Fargooo . . . please, oh, now, now, now, damn . . . damn . . . oh, God," she half-screamed, her hands pounding against his chest. She brought his rigid, pounding maleness to her, paused, and she screamed in protest, thrust herself forward over him, and he moved into her and her cry became a deep, guttural sound.

When the moment came, the hushed instant exploded again as she seemed to suspend in midair for a waiting moment, the spiral of ecstasy pausing to regather itself. Once again, her shriek filled the cabin, an absolute, total release, a scream that proclaimed the mastery of the senses above all else. When she fell back to lay panting beside him, her little smile held triumph in it, as though she had won a victory over herself. Maybe she had, he pondered as he closed his eyes, half-dozed beside her.

It was later in the day when she lay too drained to hold him beside her that he rose and dressed, went outside to see to the horses. The storm hadn't les-

sened any, the wind and snow seizing upon him as a
cat seizes on a mouse. He bent low, made his way
round the back of the cabin. The canvas roof and the
tarpaulin he'd put up were working well, the animals almost untouched by snow and wind. He fed
both horses out of the extra supply he had and
returned to the cabin as evening descended, the
swirling snow very white against the darkening sky.
Jennifer had the skillet on, warming the beef jerky,
and she'd opened a tin of beans, stirred, and set
coffee to brew, all beautifully naked.

"What happened to all that damn modesty?" he
asked.

"Went away. You did it. It'll be back for someone
else," she said. "You make a woman feel that she's
being enjoyed, appreciated."

"I'm enjoying," he said, the answer honest. Beauty
was beauty, whether it came in the shape of a mari-
gold or a maiden. He shed clothes to his shorts as he
ate and her eyes questioned. "I take off more and
you won't eat your dinner," he said.

"Conceited," she snapped. "But right."

The darkness came and he let the fire burn down to
save wood, took refuge in the bedroll again. Jennifer
was fire enough, he decided, and the night was
deep before he finally slept, his head pillowed against
her breasts.

Dawn brought more grayness, but the snow had
ceased. Wrapped in her blanket, Jennifer stood beside him as he opened the wooden square in the
wall to peer outside. The white blanket lay over
the land, turned the mountains into a deceptive picture postcard, a white lie that masked the raw dan-
gers they held in wait. "It's over," Jennifer said.

He made a harsh noise. "Hell it is, not with that
sky," he said. "It's a lull, nothing more. These storms
whirl in circles, and at the center there's a quiet
spot, pretty much as with a hurricane." He turned,
started to dress, and she shrugged off the blanket,

pulled on the long, cotton nightdress for warmth. "I'll feed the horses," he said. "Have a look around."

"What about Slattery?" she asked.

"Be damn hard to find prints now. No sense in looking, either, not till the storm's really over," he said. He paused at the door. "You stay inside. Don't go out there looking around for yourself."

"There's nothing out there now," she protested.

"Hell there isn't," Fargo snapped. "And all of it is hungry, looking to store up food."

She shot him a slightly condescending glance. "I hardly think a weasel or an ermine is going to hurt me," she said.

"Just stay the hell in here," he barked as he shut the door behind him. The freezing air caught at him at once and he peered at the leaden sky. The lull wouldn't last long, he grunted. The horses were still dry and in good shape, and he fed them, fixed a place in the tarpaulin that had come loose. He stepped out of the overhang, his eyes sweeping the whiteness below, moved in a circle to take in the peaks that rose up on all sides. The snow outlined the contours of the land and he saw that they were in a little hollow on one of the peaks, and he let his gaze sweep up the mountain. Slattery wouldn't have gone farther up, he felt certain. Not unless he had another cabin someplace he'd left off the crude map. Not impossible, Fargo grunted, yet not likely. The mountain men had little cause to build cabins any higher than this one. Trapping became too hard and too unrewarding any higher than this. Only the bighorn mountain sheep, the crafty cougars, and an occasional pack of timber wolves prowled the top mountain land. He turned his eyes from the high peaks. Slattery hadn't gone any higher, he thought again. And it was still not right, climbing this high for a temporary hideout.

He put the thought aside with the others that still demanded explanations and let his eyes move across the ground in front of him, sought signs of rabbit, deer, anything that would tell him to get the Sharps and bring down fresh meat. But the snow was still unmarked, the forest winter creatures staying burrowed or sheltered till the storm was truly past. They had their own ways of knowing. He started to turn back to the cabin when he heard the scream, Jennifer's voice, pain and terror in it. The cry had come from outside the cabin and the Colt was in his hand as he rounded the corner, skidded to a halt.

Jennifer lay on the ground, facedown, the tan buckskin jacket over her shoulders, and standing on her, crouched, teeth bared, the big Canada lynx glared up at him. Fargo saw the gray form of the rabbit nearby and the lynx's right forepaw dug into the jacket, long claws curved through the leather. Fargo moved forward, slow steps. He heard the menacing rumble well up from the lynx and the cat's light-green eyes stayed on him. He hadn't time to figure out what had happened, but to the lynx the matter was one of food, possession of prey, the most basic of all things in the fight for survival. He saw Jennifer's eyes, the side of her face pressed into the snow, terror stark in their lavender depths. He took another step closer and saw the lynx begin to arch its back, rear legs tensed. He was unwilling to back away, fifty pounds of pure power, and Fargo heard the hiss of fury that came from the cat, the wide, tufted face drawn in a snarl.

Fargo halted, froze in place. If the lynx leapt, his claws would go in deep, tearing huge chunks out of Jennifer's back. The claws of all four feet would tear into her, claws long enough to tear muscle and lay open bone. No mountain lion, the lynx was nonetheless a supremely dangerous foe, one too many people underestimated, some to their everlasting regret. There was no chance for a safe shot, he cursed silently. If he hit the big cat, the bullet could go through and into Jennifer. And in any case, the lynx would dig in and leap, the one thing he wanted most to prevent. Fargo let his voice become a harsh whisper, kept his tone steady.

"Lay still," he called softly. "No matter what I do, you lay still. Move and he'll tear your head off."

She heard him, he knew, and he met the lynx's eyes again, saw only cold determination, and the big cat's lips curled back in a snarl again. The lynx was growing more nervous and more aggressive, a leap to snatch the rabbit or to slash at him was damn close to happening. Fargo began to back away, slowly, his eyes on the cat as he moved steadily backward. The lynx watched him with unblinking, unwavering eyes, pinpoint pupils of cold fury. Fargo continued to back, reached the cabin, moved along the wall to the far corner, and backed around it. Once around the corner, he dropped to his knees, cautiously edged forward enough to let him look out past the cabin.

Jennifer lay still and he could only imagine the terror that curled inside her, but his eyes stayed on the lynx. The big cat continued to stare toward the cabin, but Fargo saw its back go down, the tightness of its hind legs lessen. He waited, the Colt raised, ready to fire if he had to, but the cat held its place on Jennifer's back and then, satisfied it was in command, its prey no longer threatened, the lynx stepped to the ground, one paw first, then another, paused to sweep the ground with a swift glance. The big cat stepped completely down from Jennifer, walked to the dead rabbit, took hold of the carcass, and slowly, disdainfully disappeared into the tamaracks.

Jennifer continued to obey his words, lay unmoving, and he holstered the Colt, trotted toward her. She lifted her head and clung to him as he pulled her to her feet. "My God," she breathed. "Oh, Jesus, I thought I was dead."

"You hurt?" he asked.

"He ripped my arm some, not bad," she said. "I

never saw him until he hit me. I fell and he slipped on the snow, or it would've been worse.''

"Goddammit, I told you to stay inside," Fargo barked as he helped her into the cabin.

"A hawk had the rabbit. I saw him and he dropped it for some reason. It was hardly marked and I thought it'd be perfect for dinner," she said.

"So did the lynx," Fargo remarked.

"I just thought to run out and bring it back," she said.

"You never just run out and pick up something. You look around first. You listen, smell, wait. You know that if you saw the hawk drop the rabbit, chances are damn good that something else saw it, something with eyes sharper than yours," he said, started to go on, and stopped. The years of learning the wild ways couldn't be passed on in words, not in any quick and easy guidebook for survival. "Just obey orders next time, dammit," he growled.

Her arm bore three slashes that might have been a lot worse, and he applied the hyssop and comfrey salve, left her to rest, and took the Sharps with him as he went outside again. The swirl of biting snow greeted him, he looked up, saw the storm's fury whistling down from the high peaks. The lull had ended with renewed fury, as it always did. He started to turn back to the cabin when he caught the movement beside two tall tamaracks. He peered through the thickening curtain, stepped closer. The almost-white form leapt into view, a big snowshoe hare. Another darted after it and he raised the Sharps, fired, and only one form continued on.

He brought the hare back, skinned it, and put it into the iron kettle to boil slowly over the fire. Snowshoe hare needed slow cooking. He'd glimpsed some wild horseradish stalks poking up through the snow, and he went back outside, pulled the roots up, and brought them in. "Make the hare taste a hell of a lot better," he said to Jennifer as he set out scraping the roots, amassed enough to put into the kettle.

She listened to the wind drive against the door. "How long?" she asked.

He shrugged. "You never know," he said. She lapsed into silence as he lay back and waited for the hare to be boiled enough. He took it out, sprinkled some more of the horseradish on it, and held it over the fire for a quick touch of searing.

"I never knew hare could be this good," Jennifer said as they ate.

"You've never been this hungry," he said. "Get hungry enough and leather tastes mighty fine."

The storm whirled against the cabin and the howl of the wind grew stronger. He saw her listen as, dinner over, she sat beside him.

"I want it to end. I want to go after Slattery," she said. "And I want it to stay, to keep you here with me with nothing else to do but make love to me."

He started to take off clothes. "Can't fight Mother Nature," he said. She whirled, was naked before he had his shorts off, almost leapt on him, her lips told him of hungers that needed no words.

He let the fire burn to embers and her screams of pleasure filled the cabin again. The night passed in her arms and morning saw the storm still raging, trees heavy with snow now, some starting to ice over. "Looks like you're going to get half of what you want," he said. He eyed her. "Little more of this and maybe you'll forget the other half," he said.

"No," she answered quickly. "No, I still want the other half. I won't be forgetting that."

He pulled her down on the bedroll with him. "You're a strange one. All kinds of things run deep inside you, don't they?" he said. "I wonder which is the real you."

She laughed. "Wonder that myself, sometimes," she said. "More now that you've made me find another part of me."

144

"I'll settle for that part," he said.

She came into his arms, nestled, content to stay quietly warm beside him.

He got her to talk some about herself during the long day, about how she'd lived growing up. Her answers were quick, unhesitating, full of names of people and places, but when he brought the conversation around to her pa and Slattery, her replies became looser, full of generalities. He turned all the little things that still stayed in his mind, decided to keep them there a spell longer.

They had some of the hare left, and with the warmed beef jerky as a side dish, it was enough for the meal. The dark came and the storm continued to rage outside, the wind so fierce it pushed through the cracks in the cabin and he kept the fire full. Jennifer pulled off clothes, stretched out on her blanket in front of the fire's warmth. The firelight bathed her in a soft yellow that echoed the glistening sparks of her hair. She turned for his eyes, enjoyed watching his enjoyment of her. It aroused her as well as him, became part of the gathering inside herself, and when he reached for her, she was aflame, her skin almost hot to the touch.

"Now, now, now," she demanded at once, and he ignored her, slowly began to caress her with his lips. He traced a burning path down her body, over the pubic mound that was softly full, pressed his face hard against the soft-firm triangle. He moved down further and she had thighs open, quivering, and he felt her hands digging into his back. "Yes," she half-screamed. "Yes, please, please, oh, Jesus, please." He brought his mouth to her and her shriek was almost as total as that final paean of abandon. He stayed with her, caressed, kissed, sucked, brought her to a new wildness, and her legs clamped around him as she screamed, held him to her as her hands dug into his shoulders. When they finally fell away, he traced the path back up along her body and she lay gasping as he caressed her breasts.

She turned suddenly, flung herself at him, reached for him, and made love again, her wild arousal contagious, beyond denying, and she seemed possessed by the need to match the new heights he had found for her. The little cabin became their world within the world again, a place apart, contained by the walls of passion and pleasure, a house of the flesh and the senses, and he was reveling in her passion when the door flew open, a swirling rush of snow billowing into the cabin.

Jennifer gave a sharp cry, more because Fargo'd pulled from her than because of the door flying open. He rose, started toward the open door, assumed an especially fierce gust had flung it open. He'd almost reached it when the figure stepped through the doorway, a monstrous apparition made of snow and ice that hung from it. Fargo stared, unsure for a moment if he were not seeing some strange beast from the snows. But the rifle pointed at him was a Winchester carbine, and it moved, motioned him back. He stepped back, saw the creature of ice and snow kick the door closed. Jennifer was on her feet, slipping the long green nightdress on.

He moved near her and she stared at the apparition. Fargo saw an ice-encrusted hat, icicles hanging from the brim. There was a face under that hat, frozen, coated with snow and ice. The figure stepped toward the fire, slow, ponderous steps of snow-covered clothes. The rifle motioned again and Fargo moved to the side, Jennifer clinging to his arm. The creature moved to the fire, placed his back to the heat of it. Slowly, the creature's head turned, saw the big Sharps standing nearby. The rifle motioned again and Fargo stepped back farther, saw his trousers near, and reached for them. The creature watched from behind eyebrows thick with ice. Fargo, trousers on, stared at the figure and saw a piece of ice fall from the hat. The tall crown of snow and ice began to melt, slip away, revealed a gray beaver hat underneath. The fire continued to quickly thaw the encrusted ice, and Fargo saw the man's brows take shape as the snow and ice fell from them. The face grew shiny as the coating of ice began to melt, drop away. He felt Jennifer's fingers dig into his arm.

"My God," she breathed. "My God. *Slattery.*"

7

Fargo stared, Jennifer's whispered gasp ringing in his ears as though it had been a shout. A large piece of packed snow fell from the man's back and shoulders to reveal a tall frame, over six feet. The man moved his arm more freely, took a step, and one leg freed itself of two inches of frozen snow. Fargo watched the coating slide from the man's face, his features take shape, a straight nose, deep-blue eyes, a hand-some-enough face.

"Slattery," he heard Jennifer gasp again, and saw the man's eyes hold on her. His lips moved and a last coating of ice fell away from his mouth.

"You," he said. "I'll be dammed." His voice little more than a rasping whisper, his eyes hard, the man turned to stare at the big figure beside Jennifer. Another large piece of hard-frozen snow fell away from the lower part of Slattery's body. He was thawing out quickly in the warm waves of heat from the fireplace at his back. It wasn't hard to put together what had happened, Fargo reflected. Slattery had left the cabin, started down, and had gotten caught in the raging storm. Fighting his way back to the cabin had obviously been his only chance.

"Damn you, Slattery," Jennifer bit out, breaking into his thoughts.

Slattery's face was free of ice now, his good looks clear, and he raised an arm, pushed his beaver hat from his head to reveal blond hair. "Goddamn," he breathed again as he stared at Jennifer. "Didn't figure you at all," he said. Every word he spoke came out shivering, and Fargo saw his body trembling despite the fire's warmth.

Fargo's glance went to the Sharps, but near frozen or not, Slattery was quick. "Don't try it, mister," he said. "This here rifle works fine." He stepped sideways, away from the fire for an instant, and Fargo saw him shiver violently as he scooped up the Sharps, emptied the shells onto the floor, and threw the rifle in a corner. He hastened back to stand against the fire again, his eyes on Jennifer. "Who's he?" he asked her.

"Fargo," she said. "I hired him to bring me after you."

"Girl wants her pa's money back," Fargo said.

Slattery stared at him for a long moment. His lips cracked wide enough to form a half-frozen grin. "Her pa's money?" he echoed. "That what she told you?"

Fargo nodded. "Don't pay attention to him," he heard Jennifer say to him, tug on his arm. "He'll say anything." Fargo nodded again, his face impassive as he wondered where truth really lay.

Slattery's face pulled tight, his eyes suddenly burning as they fixed on Jennifer. "You've been giving it to him. I listened outside. Even with the wind howlin' I could hear you," the man said, flinging words between shivers. "Bitch. Never could give it to me and now you're handing it out," he said, and Fargo saw the man's eyes turn to him, a wildness in their hatred. "You got something I don't, mister?" he rasped. "I don't like that. I don't like thinkin' someone's better than me."

Fargo kept his voice low, calming. "Better's got nothing to do with it," he said quietly. "Maybe I was just at the right place at the right time."

The man shivered, curled his lips into a snarling sneer. "No, you're at the wrong place at the wrong time, mister," Slattery said. He raised the rifle, aimed it at the big man's chest, but he directed his words at Jennifer. "I could kill him here, but that'd be too easy for him. I figure a half-naked man ought to last maybe fifteen minutes out there," he said.

"No," Jennifer gasped. "You're mad, Slattery."

The man's laugh was a half-shiver, an eerie sound. "I'm going to freeze him for you, honey," he said. "Tomorrow you can go out and see the stiffest pecker you'll ever see. You'll be able to break it off and keep it in your pocket."

"Monster," Jennifer flung at him.

"Turn around," Slattery said to Fargo.

"Now, wait a minute," Fargo tried but the man raised the rifle. "Fifteen minutes is better than nothin'," he snarled. "Turn around."

Fargo turned, his lips a hard line, and knew the utter helplessness that was his. The rifle prodded into his back.

"Start walking," Slattery said.

Fargo moved toward the door, paused as he heard the sharp sound of a blow and Jennifer's body collapsing. "That'll hold her till I get back," Fargo heard the man say, his voice shiver again. "Out, you son of a bitch," Slattery roared, and the rifle stabbed him in the back.

Fargo pulled the door open, stepped into the roaring storm, shivered instantly as the frigid wind and snow swirled around him. He stumbled forward as Slattery pushed him in the back. Fifteen minutes was an optimistic estimate, he decided. His bare skin cried out at once, each wind-driven snowflake a tiny spear. He felt his toes growing stiff instantly as he half-fell across the snow, the skin of his bare chest and back already tightening around him. The blow came from the butt of the rifle just as he had stumbled forward. It struck hard enough to send a shower of flashing lights off in his head and then the void of unconsciousness. Dimly, before he blacked out, he felt himself falling down an embankment and then the world vanished.

Only a few minutes went by before he came to, blinked his eyes open. He felt only cold—deep, embalming, numbing cold—and he saw whiteness all around him. He reached out, scratched, and the whiteness moved. He was inside a snowbank and he pulled himself to his feet. The snowbank had actually acted as insulation, keeping the freezing wind from him, the wind that would have already frozen him, dropped his body temperature in the few minutes he'd been unconscious. But the snowbank was slowly beginning to do the same in its own way, packing itself around him. He got one bare arm up, clawed the sides, and pulled himself up to the top of the bank.

The wind slammed into him at once, icy fingers that curled around his bare skin with malevolent glee. Fargo crawled forward, pushed himself to his feet. He could see the glow of the cabin, a faint light through the curtain of snow, tiny slivers escaping under the doorway. He moved toward it, no feeling in his feet any longer. If the blow had hit him squarely, kept him unconscious another five minutes, he'd have been too numb and stiff to move. As it was, he guessed he had perhaps two or three minutes more before consciousness would drift away. He could feel the slowness of his movements, a sign his body temperature was dropping fast. He could no longer feel sensation in his skin, and he moved toward the cabin in some instinctive, automatic sense, the dying creature drawn to a resting place. Slattery would have the door barricaded, he knew, but reasoning was a slow, abstract process now, no longer connected to anything but itself.

He fell on hands and knees only a few feet from the cabin, and he shook his head, fought off the numbing drowsiness that beckoned him to lie down. He brought a roar of rage from someplace deep

151

inside himself, a surge of fury that sent adrenaline pumping through his body, and he threw himself sideways, rolled, got to his feet. A moment's warmth coursed through him, inner fires, inner strengths. It would last but moments, he knew, and he peered at the cabin, saw the smoke curling up from the chimney, a gray spiral behind the swirling whiteness. He drew another shout from deep inside himself, another surge of adrenaline to course through him, and he was running on feet he could no longer feel, falling, the snow sticking to his frozen skin, pulling himself up to run again. By the rear of the cabin, by the overhang, snow had drifted high, almost to the edge of the roof. He ran onto the snowdrift, clawed his way up it with fingers that were stiffening. He reached the top, flung himself onto the roof, the blanket of snow deadening all sound beneath it. He crawled the few feet toward the chimney as he felt his strength sliding away, the numbness tightening around him. He cursed silently as his motion halted, drew on a final burst of rage, pulled himself forward again.

His hand reached out, touched the stones. Heat, merciful, consuming heat. He pressed his palm against the stone, held it there, and felt the warmth slowly move down his wrist, into his forearm, enough to let him pull himself forward again. He fell against the chimney stones, pressed his bare chest to them. Because of the frigid wind and snow, they were warm, not scalding, and he felt his blood begin to flow, his chest heave, skin become alive. He turned his back to the stones, pressed it against their heat, drew his legs up, let the blessed warmth flow through his bare body. The packed snow fell away from his trousers and he could feel his groin tingle as the blood flowed through him. He swung his legs up to the flat stones that formed the top of the low chimney, and he lay across their warmth as the smoke curled into the air beside him.

The snow fell on him, but his body was warm now, stayed warm as the heated stones transmitted their comfort to him, and the snow melted almost as quickly as it touched him. He turned on his stomach and let the warmth draw through him from the front.

The glow of the fire rose halfway up the chimney. Slattery had put more wood on and Fargo found a grim smile as the added heat rose through the stones to bring him more of its life-giving warmth. The flat-topped stones were no bed of comfort, yet they were not the worst place he'd ever lain on; he curled onto his side on their warmth, turned frequently, felt a little like an egg on a grill. But he was alive—all but naked in the raging storm, yet alive. He caught Slattery's voice suddenly, rising up through the chimney with the smoke. The man was obviously standing close to the fireplace and Fargo heard the shiver still on his voice.

"You'll stay tied nice and tight till morning, honey," Fargo heard the man say. "I'll be thawed and rested some by then, be able to show you what Jack Slattery can give you." He heard the man say something else, but the words drifted away as Slattery stepped back from the fireplace.

He'd thrown another log on and Fargo felt the added warmth rise up. He turned on his other side, began to think ahead. Morning would come soon enough. Sooner or later Slattery would emerge from the cabin to find his frozen form. The man would walk in confidence, never thinking to look up. Fargo's eyes narrowed in thought. He couldn't risk battling with Slattery. Once away from the hot stones, the icy cold would seize him at once and Slattery would be armed.

Fargo's thoughts raced, formed the one plan that could work. He would pounce as the cougar pounces, one swift, flying leap. It had to give him time to get into the cabin, behind the walls that would protect

153

him from Slattery's bullets and the cold that would act instantly upon his near nakedness. He lay back on the warm stones, half-dozed, suddenly woke, aware that his face felt dry.

He sat up against the chimney. The snow had stopped, the wind ceased its furious howling. He leaned back against the warmth of the chimney and dozed again, was awake when morning came, a winter sun nudging itself over the high mountain peaks. It crept over the lone, almost naked figure on the roof of the little cabin, and Fargo realized that without the warm chimney stones, the sun would merely delay his freezing to death. He waited, heard the mumble of voices from the bottom of the chimney, stayed against the warm stones.

His eyes swept the land, deep in its pristine mantle, but it was the stillness that caught at him, a total, absolute stillness where nothing moved, called, cried. In time, the winter creatures would stir, find their way through the snow, seek out prey, food, shelter. But now they stayed huddled away from the power of nature's fury. Now there was only stillness, deep, total.

It was midmorning when he heard the door being pulled open, Slattery's voice drifting up the roof. "Come on, bitch, follow me. Or do I have to bring him back to you?" Fargo heard the man say, a harsh laugh following his words.

Fargo rose to a crouch, left the warmth of the chimney stones to move to the edge of the roof. He felt the snow and cold clutch at him instantly, his bare skin trembling. Slattery's tall frame strode from the cabin below him and Fargo saw the man carried the Winchester and the Sharps. Probably a handgun, too, he guessed. He gathered all the power in his thigh muscles, shook away the penetrating cold that stabbed deeply. He leapt, feetfirst, came down to strike Slattery in the back with both feet. The man shouted in surprise more than pain as he flew forward, sprawled a half-dozen feet in the snow.

Fargo landed on his side on the snow-covered ground, rolled, raced for the cabin door, and saw Jennifer there, her eyes wide with shock. He dived past her through the doorway, hit the floor, and rolled as the bullet hurtled through after him, slammed into the wall. He turned, glimpsed Jennifer slam the door shut with her shoulder as another shot thudded into it. He ran to it, used a length of the firewood to barricade the door.

Slattery roared in fury outside, fired another round of bullets in frustrated rage that slammed harmlessly into the cabin.

Fargo turned from the door and Jennifer flung herself into his arms. "I thought you were dead," she breathed. "I still don't believe it."

"Believe it," he said grimly.

She drew back, stared at him. "How?" she asked. "You're practically naked. How?"

"Chimneys are wonderful things," he said. "I never knew how wonderful till last night."

Her eyes grew wider. "You were on the roof, by the chimney?"

He nodded. "But I almost never made it that far," he said.

Slattery's roar from outside cut off her questions. "You're dead, both of you, you hear me? You're dead," the man shouted.

"He may be right. He has both rifles and your Colt. He even found my little pistol and took it," she said. "He'll wait to pick us off the minute we try to leave, and we don't have food or firewood to stay in here forever."

Fargo drew his empty holster on and sat down, felt the weariness in his every muscle. He stretched, got to his feet again, turned to Jennifer, and his eyes were hard. "We'll get out of here. Don't know how far we'll get after that. But first you're going to level with me, all the way," he said.

She frowned. "I don't know what you mean," she said.

His arm shot out, his hand closing around the front of the long green nightdress. He yanked her forward, almost off her feet. "You goddamn well know what I mean. I want the truth about this whole business. You've been lying from the very start," he rasped.

"Lying?" she said, looked hurt. "How can you say that?"

"Easy. You offered me a thousand dollars out of your savings. Hell, honey, you haven't lived long enough to save a thousand dollars, not even if you were a dance-hall girl," he said.

"I made a mistake, used the wrong word. It wasn't savings. It was money left to me," she said.

He grunted. "Fast thinking, but no sale. You said Slattery stole a lot of money, a real bundle. It has to be, for all the fuss over it. But your pa spent his life as a haulage wagon driver. Where'd a haulage driver get that kind of money? It doesn't fit, no way. And last night Slattery laughed when he heard the story you gave me. Now I want the truth or I'll get myself out of here and leave you and Slattery to each other."

"You wouldn't do that," she said.

"Don't bet on it," he growled. "I want the truth. You talk or I walk."

She glowered at him. "I wasn't lying about the money. He ran off with it, over twenty thousand dollars," Jennifer said

"Only it wasn't your pa's money and that story about him financing Slattery to make maps is phony as a three-dollar bill," Fargo snapped. "Where'd the money come from?"

She looked at him from under frowning brows, the defensive anger in her eyes. "The Cheyenne

Wells Bank," she murmured, and Fargo felt his own brows lift.

"The Cheyenne Wells bank?" he echoed. "Slattery stole it?" She nodded. "Where do you come into it?" he questioned.

"I worked at the bank. It was payroll money and I knew when it'd be there. I was the inside one, I let him in. Without me, it would never have happened. He'd have never gotten in himself. We were supposed to split it, he and I, fifty-fifty," she said.

"Davis? Where does he fit in?" Fargo pressed.

"He and three other men helped Slattery pull the actual robbery after I let them in. They blew the safe, and when the sheriff got there, I was on the floor, fainted dead away," she told him. "Nobody ever suspected I was in on it. Slattery was supposed to split his half with Davis and the others."

"But he ran out on all of you," Fargo mused aloud. "That's why they didn't want me helping you. They wanted to get to him first themselves."

"But I had the map he'd left behind," Jennifer said almost smugly.

Fargo gave her a narrowed glance. "Lied about all of it, the whole damn story one big lie," he said.

"Couldn't help it." Jennifer shrugged.

"You're as good at making excuses for yourself as you are at making up stories," he snapped.

The sweet-violet eyes met his gaze without wavering. "Would you have helped me if I'd told you I was after stolen bank money?" she asked, the question's simple logic its own answer.

"Guess not," he conceded. "Doesn't excuse your lying to me."

"I never had anything, Fargo. All that money, and all I had to do was help them get in. I went along with it. Maybe I even looked up to Jack Slattery. He was handsome and kind of sweet-talking," she said.

"He's not sweet-talking now," Fargo commented.

"No, maybe he's gone off with the money now

that the storm's over," she said. "If so, we can follow him. I still want that money. I did my part of it and it's half mine."

"None of it's yours, honey," Fargo said harshly. "It belongs to the bank and all those poor slobs who put their hard-earned money there to be safe." She turned away, made no reply, her brows knitted. "Besides, he hasn't got it with him," Fargo said.

Jennifer's head swiveled to him, her eyes widening. "How do you know that? He could have a sack tied to his horse or have it spread into his saddlebags," she said.

Fargo shook his head. "It never set right. Man climbs this high into these mountains to hide out, he means to stay. But Slattery never meant to stay. The cabin's not stocked for it. He came, holed up a week or two, and started down the other side just before we got here. He'd have kept going if the storm hadn't caught him. He had to get back here if he wanted to stay alive."

"What are you saying?" Jennifer asked.

"He came here to hide the money and then leave. He figured to hole up someplace safer and come back for it, in the spring, I'd guess," Fargo said, and saw her eyes grow wide.

"You mean the money's right here in this cabin someplace?" she exploded.

"Someplace," he said.

Her eyes went down to the wide pine planks that formed the floor of the cabin. "Under there someplace," she said.

"Maybe," he answered. "They'll lift up easy enough."

She knelt down at once, wedged fingers between the planks, and he helped her pull the center one up. The soil beneath it lay pressed flat, its surface almost smooth. It was soil that plainly hadn't been disturbed in years, soil that would easily reveal new shovel marks. They put the plank down as they

158

lifted the adjoining one, the earth beneath it exactly the same. It didn't take long to uncover each board of the small cabin floor, and the last one proved to be the same as the first, the soil beneath undisturbed.

Jennifer's face showed angry disappointment. "Outside someplace," she muttered. "He could've buried it anyplace out there. We'd never find it except by luck, and surely not with him out there waiting to pick us off."

Fargo's lips pursed in thought. "No, not outside," he said slowly.

"Why not?" Jennifer questioned almost angrily.

"He wouldn't have come way the hell up here to do that. There are a million places lower down in the mountains if he wanted to bury it under a tree or a rock somewhere," Fargo said. "It's in here, in this cabin somewhere."

"Where? There's no place else. The walls are solid log," she answered, and her eyes went to the low roof. "Nothing I can see up there but log. Unless it's on top of the roof someplace," Jennifer said. A frown crossed her forehead as she watched Fargo pick up an iron fireplace poker, step to one side of the fireplace. He started at the base, tapped the lowest stone, listened to the dull, solid sound of it. He went to the next, did the same, and again listened to the heavy solid sound.

Jennifer's eyes were round, hope and excitement in them as she watched him go from stone to stone, up the one side of the fireplace and on to the stones that formed the chimney. He stopped midway up the face of the chimney and began again at the base of the other side. The hope in Jennifer's eyes had dimmed somewhat, he noted. He had reached halfway up the second row of the chimney stones when he halted, tapped the oblong stone again.

It rang rather than thudded as all the others had. The others, solid against each other, absorbed sound at once. This one let sound ring against it. He put the poker down, grasped the stone, pulled on it, and felt it move. He took a better hold, pulled it from the side, and the stone slid out of its place.

Jennifer was reaching one arm deep into the hole at once, pulled back, and he saw her bring the canvas sack out, swing it onto the table. She pulled the top open almost frantically and he heard the hiss of triumph that came from her.

He peered into the sack to see the bundles of United States currency, met Jennifer's eyes. "We found it, we've got it," she breathed. "Oh, Jesus, Fargo, we've got it." Her arms went around him in a swift hug.

"Now all we have to do is get out of here alive with it," he said, but the problem didn't take away the glee in her face as she stared into the sack again.

"Mine, all of it," she said, lifted her eyes to him. "Ours," she said.

"We'll talk about that later," he told her as he pushed the rock back in place. "Now simmer down, relax. We've nothing to do but wait for night."

She took the sack with her as she moved to her blanket. "What are you thinking?" she asked

"Our only chance to get out of here is by night. It's going to get damn cold sitting quietly out there, and he can't stay awake twenty-four hours a day. By dark he's going to have to keep moving if he doesn't want to freeze to death, and he's going to be damn tired," Fargo said.

"Maybe we ought to wait another night," she said. "He'll be even colder and more tired."

"And we'll be one day closer to another storm. There's one coming, you can count on it. They follow each other all winter long, sometimes only a day apart, sometimes a week. There's no telling, but we've got to be as far down as we can before the next one hits," he told her, and she nodded gravely. "He'll see our tracks, come morning, easy to follow in the snow. If we've enough of a head start, maybe we'll have a chance," Fargo said. "No fire tonight. Now I'm going to get some sleep. We'll be riding through the night."

He stretched out on the bedroll and the tiredness swept over him at once. He was asleep in seconds, woke when the cabin began to grow cold, and he crawled under the bedroll, saw Jennifer asleep under the blanket. The cabin was pitch-black when he woke again, and he whispered her name, heard her come awake. "Get your things on," he said. "Time to move out."

He found his own clothes in the dark, heard her groping through the stygian blackness. "Ready," she whispered finally, and he felt along the wall till he reached the door. He pulled it open a fraction. A half-moon reflected off the snow to make the night entirely too bright, and he cursed softly, pushed the door open a few inches more.

"Crawl," he hissed, dropped to his hands and knees, and slipped through the narrow opening of the doorway. He stayed against the cabin as he made his way toward the overhang at the rear, paused once to peer across the snow, saw nothing, and moved on. Once behind the tarpaulin, he rose to his feet, saddled the Ovaro, and waited for Jennifer to finish. He stayed in place as she mounted, his eyes skyward, and he saw the clouds move over the half-moon to leave only a dim white over the land. He moved out from beneath the canvas roof, circled back to the other side of the mountain, grateful for the thickness of the snow that deadened the sound of hooves.

They were well into the trees, moving downward, when the moon came out again. He saw the land going downhill with no precipitous drop-offs, but he kept the horses moving slowly. From the position of the moon he estimated they'd have a good four or five hours' head start before dawn. Maybe more, he grunted. Maybe Slattery wouldn't notice the door of the cabin ajar till the sun came up. He glanced at Jennifer. No apprehension on her face, only excitement, the canvas sack tied to her saddle horn. She was spending the money already, he reckoned.

They made good time, the back of the mountain much easier riding than the front. "You think Davis and his men are still following our old trail?" Jennifer asked.

"Not likely. I'd say they headed back down fast when the first storm broke," he said, looked up as a faint line of pink edged the top of the peaks.

"Morning," Jennifer said, following his glance.

"We keep going as long as we can," he said.

The sun rose quickly to turn the whiteness into a glare and Fargo saw the flash of a black-tailed deer a dozen yards away. They had come almost six hours down from the high mountain land. The mountain slopes would hold plenty of forest life now, predator and prey, the battle for survival in full swing. As if to echo his thoughts, he glimpsed a distant grizzly standing atop a mound of snow, his rich brown coat glistening in the sun.

Fargo halted as he saw the land drop off sharply, a deep slope, but at the bottom of it there was a line of rock and balsams. "Follow me, slow and easy," he said as he started the Ovaro down the slope sideways, let the snow kick up to form a cushion, and the horse slide downward to the bottom. He saw Jennifer come after him, the bay having an easier time of it because of the snow kicked up by the Ovaro.

He led the way along the line of rocks, found two that formed a semicave protected by three tall balsams, and he slid from the saddle, pulled out his bedroll, and sank into it, tiredness gripping every part of his body.

Jennifer came in beside him, was asleep in seconds. He lay awake a moment longer. Six hours' start, he pondered. Maybe. Slattery would catch up to them sooner or later. He'd move faster following their trail. Fargo's jaw tightened. He had to find a spot to make a stand by then, find a way to meet a man armed with two rifles, two six-guns, and a pistol with only a thin-bladed throwing knife. He let sleep shut away the prospect.

the trees. The moon rose quickly and there came
light enough to move things at a good pace. He
was first to see the silent shapes that melted

8

He woke as dusk began to settle in, crawled from
the bedroll, and let Jennifer gather herself. His eyes
peered back up the way they'd come, but it was
habit and built-in caution. Slattery wouldn't be this
close yet. He'd have to stop and rest some, and they
could stretch their lead a few hours again. He climbed
onto the Ovaro and set out, Jennifer riding close behind him. Night and the half-moon came to reflect
on the snow and turn the night into a kind of half-
day. He called a rest after a few hours to eat some of
the hardtack in Jennifer's bag, and mountain grasses
pushed up through a thin spot in the snow, enough
for the horses to graze.

"You're very quiet," Jennifer commented. "We've
got the money. We've got a good head start. You
ought to be happy."

"You're happy enough for both of us," he growled,
finished his hardtack, and swung onto the Ovaro.
He increased the pace a little, but only a little. The
snow could hide sudden holes, slides, a hundred
unpleasant surprises. But the mountain smiled on
them and the terrain sloped downward without impossible places to overcome. It would be a long trip
around the base of the mountain when they reached
the bottom, he knew, but he'd wrestle with that
when the time come.

He rode through the morning when it came, finally halted in the thick of an oak forest. They slept till
he woke once again with the dusk sliding through

the trees. The moon rose quickly and the forest grew light enough to move through at a good pace. He was first to see the silent shapes that suddenly materialized in the night, fading in and out of the trees like so many gray wraiths. He heard Jennifer's quick cry of alarm when she became aware of them.

"Wolves, Fargo," she gasped out.

"Been moving along with us for a good half-hour," he said.

She drew her horse up beside him. "Are they going to attack us?" she asked. "God, we haven't even got a gun."

"Not tonight," he said.

She cast an angry glance at him. "How can you be so damn sure?" she snapped.

"The night's damn near over, for one thing," he said. "Then they're just running alongside, looking us over. They do love horseflesh, but they're not going to do any thing now. When a wolf pack aims to attack, they move differently. You can see it, feel it. Just keep riding."

She stayed alongside him as they moved on, apprehension in her face that only left when the wolves disappeared as suddenly as they had come. The morning slid down the mountainside, and he found a campsite and slept quickly; he woke in the late afternoon, but the sun was still bright. He rose, stood against a tree, and peered back up the mountainside; his jaw turned hard. The lone horseman stood out boldly against the snow, moving fast down the slope in their tracks. Fargo swore aloud. Slattery had done with less sleep than he'd expected, made excellent time. He turned away as Jennifer woke.

"Let's ride," he said. "Company's coming."

Fear swept her face at once and she practically flew into the saddle. Fargo paused a moment longer to stare at their tracks in the snow. There was no way to disguise them, not without things that would take too long to find. He mounted up and sent the Ovaro on in a fast trot.

Slattery would be damn close by dark, he knew, spurred on by the freshness of their tracks. He might even have caught a glimpse of orange-red hair. Fargo swore and kept riding, welcomed the dark as it came. But the forest offered no place to hide, make a stand, try to outwit their pursuer, and he rode on grimly. A sudden wailing call broke into his thoughts, echoed by another, close at hand. The gray shapes materialized again, ghostly shadows, and Jennifer rode close beside him.

"I know, they're just looking us over," she said.

"They did that last night," he said, and saw the fear leap into her eyes. She peered at him, saw the hard line of his face. His eyes flicked to the gray shapes moving on both sides of them. "Look at them," he slid at her. "They're not trotting along. They're loping now."

"They're going to attack," she breathed.

"Not for a while yet. It's part of their tactics. They run their prey, exhaust it physically. But they do more. They bring it to the edge of panic. An animal run by a wolf pack will often be so frightened it makes mistakes, its sense of survival knocked out of shape."

"We're not racing. They can't physically exhaust us," she said.

"They will. We'll have to make a run for it sooner or later. They're edging closer now. It's all we can do. Sometimes they'll break off the chase," he told her, and saw her eyes grasp at the hope in his words. He didn't tell her the rest. There'd be no outracing the pack in the snow, and the wolves wouldn't break off with the certainty of a kill in front of them. He watched the gray shapes move in closer, lope along, drift off, come back again. They made countless dry runs. It was their way, measuring, calculating, waiting, measuring again. He thought

166

he had the pack leader picked out, a huge gray wolf with a white collar that stayed always a few paces in front of the others. Fargo caught a glimpse of yellow eyes that flashed, then vanished.

"Slattery," Jennifer said. "How close is he?"

"Close enough, I'd guess," Fargo said. "Maybe a quarter of a mile back by now."

"He'll hear them. Maybe he'll help us," Jennifer said, desperation flinging aside logic.

"Why?" Fargo said coldly. "He'll let them do us in. They're not going to eat the money."

She fell silent and Fargo felt the frown suddenly dig at him, the thought blaze inside him. Once the pack attacked, they were finished. Even with weapons, standing off a good-sized wolf pack was damn hard. They had no chance of outrunning them, even though he'd have to try. The thought took on shape inside him. Their only chance was to keep them from attacking, throw them another prey, inflame the killing lust that was built into them. It was the only chance left. If it failed, they were done for anyway. If he could make it work, they would see the sun come up.

"You take these," he said to Jennifer, handing her the Ovaro's reins. She stared at him, frowned as she took the reins from his hand. "Keep at a nice trot just the way we are, keep the horses together. I'm getting off," he said.

"You're what?" she gasped.

"We've one chance. I'm going to take it," he said. "There's no time to explain now. You keep riding. If you see them disappear, you can stop. If not, ride like hell . . . and good luck."

"Fargo!" she called as he slid from the saddle, dropped to one knee on the ground. He saw her face as she looked back at him, terror in every line of it. But she kept on, held the Ovaro close to the bay. He stayed motionless as the gray shapes moved after her. They'd not noticed him, their concentration on the two horses.

He let them go out of sight before he rose, slipped to one side, and positioned himself against a tree. He drew the thin, double-edged throwing knife from its holster around his calf, had just taken it in hand when he saw the horseman coming through the trees.

Slattery rode at a fast trot, his eyes peering ahead. Fargo cursed at the man as he neared. Slattery was layered in clothing. The knife would hardly penetrate most of it, certainly nothing vital. Slattery was almost abreast of him. It had to be a variation of his leap from the rooftop, no attempt to do battle, a quick strike to accomplish what had to be done. He moved forward, crouched, every muscle tensed, the blade held ready to strike downward.

Slattery reached the tree, started past, and Fargo leapt out from the side. He plunged the knife into the man's leg, drew it down from the hip almost to the knee, a long, slicing cut. As Slattery shouted in pain and surprise, Fargo flung himself aside and glimpsed the blood spurt from the man's leg.

"Goddamn," Slattery roared, reined up, wheeled the horse, fired the rifle across his lap. Fargo dived into the trees as the bullets slammed bits of wood into his face. Slattery wheeled the horse again, charged after him, firing, and Fargo ducked from tree to tree, stayed behind cover, and saw Slattery halt, stare down at his leg, which had turned red with blood.

He saw the man's head lift, stare into the trees. It hadn't taken long, the scent of the blood drifting through the clear night air in seconds. Slattery saw the gray shapes moving through the trees toward him, and the full impact of it dawned on him.

"You goddamn bastard," the man roared, "you son-of-a-bitch bastard." He fired a raging volley of shots, a wild, stupid gesture of rage.

Fargo saw him turn his horse, fire another volley of wild shots at the wolves that came in from all sides now, the bloody leg a beacon, inflaming, setting off the lust to kill. Fargo drew back as he saw Slattery try to make a run for it. He made perhaps a half-dozen yards when two wolves seized his horse at the left hind leg. The horse screamed, went down in the rear. Three more gray shapes hurtled into the horse's neck and Fargo saw Slattery fall. The man tried to get to his feet, but his sliced leg collapsed. A few of the wolves stayed on the horse, the others leapt at the bloody prey in front of them.

Fargo saw Slattery fire, bring down one gray form, fire again wildly, miss. A wolf slammed into him, fangs flashing, crushing jaws snapping Slattery's forearm in two. The man disappeared beneath the gray bodies and Fargo heard the tearing sounds and the snapping of killing jaws. And he heard Slattery's screams, only a few, all cut short, then a guttural cry and then nothing but the growling, slavering sounds of flesh being torn apart.

Fargo sank down behind the tree. They would finish man and horse, enough for the pack for at least one day, and they'd vanish into the night, satisfied, no threat till hunger sent them searching once more. Fargo waited, forced himself to shut out the sounds, and finally there was silence. He heard a howl, in the distance yet close enough. He rose, picked his way through the strewn remains, found Slattery's almost unrecognizable body. He found what he searched for in the snow, his Sharps and the big Colt. He picked them up and hurried away, broke into his long, loping stride, not unlike the lope of a wolf.

He spotted Jennifer finally where she had halted. She dropped out of the saddle as he came up, her arms encircling him. "It's over," he said.

"They just disappeared suddenly," she said. "I heard the shooting."

"I gave them Slattery," he said. "Just as he'd have hung back and watched them tear us apart." It wasn't an apology, she realized, just the harshness of survival and truth.

They reached the base of the mountain in two more days of steady riding, nature holding back. The snows would be hard here if they came, but not with the fury of the high mountain passes. Fargo started the long trail from the back of the mountain, around the base, to bring them out in the direction they had first started. It was the end of the fourth day when they reached the start of the direct trail back. He'd made camp, a little fire burning as the sun began to sink.

"I figure we can be in Cheyenne Wells in another week or so," he said.

Jennifer's frown was instant. "Cheyenne Wells? Whatever for?" she said.

"To turn that money back to the bank," he said.

"You're out of your mind," she answered.

"I'm sure they've got a reward posted for it. Probably two thousand. That's a nice piece of change. Could take a girl far," he said.

"Not as far as twenty thousand," she snapped.

"That money belongs to a lot of hardworking people," he sighed.

"It belongs to me now. I never had anything; I've got it and I'm keeping it," she said.

"Sooner or later someone's going to realize you were part of it. You'll be looking over your shoulder the rest of your life. You don't want that," he said.

"I'll go where I won't have to look over my shoulder," she said adamantly.

He sighed wearily. "Can't let you do that to yourself," he said. "I'm taking the money back, honey." He reached out, lifted the sack from around her saddle horn. "Sorry, it's the best thing you can do, even though you don't see it now."

"I won't see it later either," she flung back. "You give me that money, damn you, Fargo."

"Stolen money will bring you no good," he said.

"Don't you be sanctimonious with me. I want that money. I'll take my chances on how much good it'll do me," she said.

"It's going back. We'll make up a good story for the sheriff and the bank in Cheyenne Wells," he said.

"I thought you and I, Fargo, hell, we'd have the world together. We fit, you know how great it was between us," she said.

"It was great, but the money goes back," he said.

She turned away, put her back to him, and he laid out his bedroll, undressed, and she finally turned back. "Maybe you're right," she said contritely. "Maybe I just got carried away with myself." She came to him, put her hands on his chest. "But you can't say for sure what'll happen in Cheyenne Wells when I bring the money back."

"It'll go well," he interrupted.

"You can't say for sure," she said. "I want one thing now, Fargo. I want you to make love to me again. Christ, I want that. No matter what happens, I want that."

Her hands moved down, slid under his shorts, pulled the garment down. She dropped to her knees, pressed her face against his organ, and he felt it respond at once, grow, blossom for her lips. She made love to him with the wildness that was always inside her, everything that had been before and something added, a desperation that gave a new dimension to her ecstasy. She made him come with her kisses, her lips, refused to be put off, and then she drew him into her, let her warmth bring him to another erection, and she screamed and shrieked and stayed with his every thrust, hanging on longer than he'd ever seen her do before; and when she finally climaxed, she carried him with her, her scream trailing off across the forests.

He lay back, drained, satisfied from head to toe, and the little smile edged his lips as she nestled against him. He stayed as she sat up finally, full rounded breasts swaying so beautifully together as she half-turned, reached behind her. He saw her turn back, and the big Colt .45 was in her hands as she drew back, stepped out of the bedroll.

"I want the money, Fargo," she said. "Dammit, I'm going to take it."

"More surprises, Jennifer?" he said.

"I wanted it my way, you and I together, but you want to play Mister Goody-two-shoes," she said.

"It's not that. There are just some things I don't go for. Stealing's one of them," he said.

She held the gun steady on him. "Taking my money is one more you won't be doing," Jennifer snapped.

"Never had a naked gal pull my own gun on me," he said. "I'm trying to decide if I like it."

She took another step backward, pulled her skirt on with one hand, then the blouse, but the Colt never wavered. "That better?" she tossed at him.

"Can't say that it is." He smiled, drew his shorts on, his trousers next.

She watched him put his shirt on, frowned, eyed her horse behind him. He saw her decide she'd have to come too close to him to reach the brown mare.

"Get the money and toss it over here," she said.

His smile was tinged with disappointment. "Can't do that, honey," he said as he turned, walked to the Ovaro.

"Fargo!" she screamed. "Don't make me," she said.

He put his hand on the sack. "It's going back," he said.

"Damn you, Fargo, damn you," he heard her scream. He started to lift the sack from the mare

172

when he heard the sharp click of the hammer on an empty chamber. He turned, saw her stare at the gun, her mouth open.

"I figured you for this kind of stunt. I took the bullets out before I made camp," he said.

She looked up at him, threw the empty gun at him, and he caught it before it hit the ground. "I didn't want to do it, damn you," she screamed.

"You didn't really want to kill Clare either. You had second thoughts. Didn't stop you from trying, though," he said, his voice becoming steel. "You'd have had second thoughts just now, too, I'm sure. But they wouldn't have stopped you either." She stared at him. "You've the conscience of an eel, honey, it keeps twisting and turning."

"Go to hell, Fargo," she screamed at him.

He took the canvas sack and swung onto the Ovaro, hung the sack over the saddle horn. "You coming?" he asked, looked down at her.

"Where?" she spit out.

"To hell," he said. "But I'm stopping off at Cheyenne Wells first."

He rode on slowly, heard her mount up and come after him. He glanced back. She rode a half-dozen paces behind. He smiled inwardly. She'd stay. Two thousand was a lot better than nothing. He'd come to know Jennifer Carlyle pretty damn well. She'd take the reward and come wanting for one more. He wouldn't deny a lady one more reward.

LOOKING FORWARD!

**The following is the opening section
from the next novel in the exciting
Trailsman series from Signet:**

THE TRAILSMAN #30
WHITE SAVAGE

*The Black Hills in Dakota Territory in the early 1860's,
the land of the Cheyenne, Blackfoot, and Pawnee,
tribes uniting now under the mad but inspired leadership
of a renegade cavalry officer . . .*

There were at least twenty Cheyenne warriors.

On a distant ridge, they sat their ponies in single file, the scalps on their lances tugging in the wind.

All this Skye Fargo saw in a single glance. As he directed his gaze straight ahead, he kept his pinto to a steady trot and did not look to his right a second time. He did not need to look again. He knew the Cheyenne weren't going anywhere—and when they did, they sure as hell wouldn't be riding in the other direction. They were all dressed for a scalping party, and Fargo was the one who had shown up.

Peering into the low sun, Fargo saw the valley's

grassy floor stretching ahead of him unbroken for miles. To his left, however, rose a small bluff, and beyond that Fargo glimpsed the peaks and buttes of broken country, the badlands. If Fargo could reach that mean country, he just might keep his scalp.

Keeping his weight forward in the stirrups to save the pinto, he edged the horse to his left and pushed his hat brim forward in a gesture calculated to appear casual to the watching Cheyenne. Moving his head only slightly to the right, he peered out from under the hat brim and saw the Cheyenne still perched on the ridge—as motionless as stone, watching, waiting.

To a casual observer, one glancing up at Fargo in a hurry in a dark place perhaps, it might have appeared that a bear unaccountably dressed in a wide-brimmed hat and loose-fitting buckskins had dropped upon the back of the pinto and now prowled above it, aping a white man. For Fargo was a giant of a man, huge in the shoulder and narrow in the gut, with a face cut from granite and softened only by a pair of lake-blue eyes—eyes that never failed to draw a woman, any woman he wanted.

The night before, after a full evening of storming through raucous saloons and gambling halls, he had found himself a wench to his taste, a raven-haired dance-hall girl he had immediately liberated. As he soon found to his delight in the privacy of his room, she was a girl who appreciated his hungers and presented him with a few of her own for him to satisfy. Now, as he rode under the grim gaze of those Cheyenne warriors, the thought of last night's carousal warmed his gut and reminded him that there were still women he had not yet plowed and towns he had not yet explored—and a murderous bunch of cutthroats he had yet to track down.

Still edging his pinto to the left, he stole another glance at the ridge. The Indians were almost behind him now, the closest they would get without moving from the ridge. At that moment a cavalry officer suddenly appeared on the ridge beside the Cheyenne. As Fargo watched in amazement, the officer raised a saber over his head, then swung it down, its blade flashing in the sunlight.

The Cheyenne swept off the ridge in a single wave.

Hauling his pinto hard to the left, Fargo bent low over its neck and slapped its rump, letting out a blood curdling yell as he did so. That was all the pinto needed. It bounded into a dead run on its first leap, its legs a blinding blur as the horse raced toward the bluff.

Fargo turned in his saddle and took in at a single glance the storm of Cheyenne coming on now at a full gallop. They rode easily and gracefully, not yelling or waving their arms needlessly. A strangely quiet, surprisingly well-disciplined war party, Fargo realized. He turned back around and saw four Indians approaching from his left, and two more converging on him from the right. The Cheyenne on the ridge had caught his attention, lulled him, and now they were driving him into a pincers.

He decided his best bet was to go for the smaller war party. Drawing his Colt, he thumbed back the hammer, waited for a good shot, then picked off the closest Cheyenne. As the brave tumbled backward off his paint, Fargo swung the Ovaro directly for the dead Cheyenne's companion, aimed, and fired a second time. This shot missed as the Cheyenne—still riding toward him at full gallop—hauled up his flintlock and fired. The round whistled over Fargo's head. Before the Cheyenne could reload, Fargo was on him, and with one vicious swipe of his revolver he knocked the savage off his pony.

With the other four Cheyenne in hot pursuit, Fargo swept on past the downed Cheyenne. Bending low over the pinto, he looked back, brought up his Colt, and fired twice. His second round caught the lead Cheyenne's pony in the chest. As the animal plunged into the ground, the horse and rider behind him stumbled headlong over the thrashing horse.

Fargo turned around and a moment later reached the bottom of the bluff. Without pausing, he urged the Ovaro on up the steep slope. In great leaping bounds, the pinto scrambled toward the crest. The shale under the pinto's hooves was treacherous, but a wide game trail opened before him, and up this the pinto bounded, Fargo standing in the stirrups now, leaning far out over the plunging animal's head. A storm of arrows flew past. One nicked his right arm and glanced harmlessly off.

Just before he reached the top of the bluff, he glanced back to see the entire Cheyenne war party scrambling up the slope after him. In that single swift glance, he saw clearly their stoic, savage faces, each of them covered with war paint.

But he did not see the cavalry officer.

Fargo looked back around just as the pinto burst over the crest of the slope and saw three more Cheyenne warriors charging across the bluff toward him. They were only about five galloping paces away, and before the pinto planted its hind hooves for its first stride, Fargo shot the closest Cheyenne in the neck. Charging the next one, he fired again, his slug catching the Cheyenne's horse under the jaw. The pony reared over backward, screaming in pain. The Indian almost threw himself clear, but one leg was caught under the pony as it slammed to the ground. Rolling and kicking wildly, the pony thrashed its head and crunched down on the Cheyenne's skull, flattening it.

The remaining Cheyenne was armed with a rifle. As Fargo charged toward him, the brave fired. Fargo ducked low and felt the slug slam into his saddle. It felt as if someone had struck it with a sledgehammer. Returning the Cheyenne's fire point-blank, Fargo missed. It was too late by this time to thumb-cock his revolver. Charging straight at the Cheyenne, Fargo bowled into the Cheyenne's paint. The shock of the collision momentarily stopped both horses. They reared in confusion. As the pinto came down, Fargo ripped the rifle from the Cheyenne's hands, then poked the barrel of his Colt into his midsection and blew a hole in him. As the Cheyenne spilled from his horse, Fargo slapped the pinto's rear and raced on toward the badlands.

Behind him, the Cheyenne war party crested the rim of the bluff. Their discipline until now had been remarkable, but the sight of their dead comrades caused a few of them to let loose with bloodcurdling war cries. A moment later, the air was rent as the entire war party let loose. The sound was enough to cause the Ovaro to surge ahead just a bit faster.

Fargo aimed the pinto at the looming rocks and crags that marked the beginning of the badlands. Reaching a massive boulder, Fargo disappeared behind it and followed a trail leading to higher ground. His horse was now laboring, but Fargo had no choice; he had to keep the Ovaro going. When he reached the higher ground, he flung himself from the horse and tethered it out of sight behind some rocks. Snaking his Sharps from its scabbard, he raced back a few yards and ducked down behind a clump of rimrocks for cover.

Spreading a handful of cartridges on a flat rock beside him, he bellied down and watched the oncoming Cheyenne. Strung out in a ragged line, in full cry now, they were streaming through the badlands toward his rocky redoubt. Fargo levered the trigger guard, breaking open the Sharps' chamber. He slipped a cartridge into the chamber and pulled the trigger guard closed. Then he wedged the stock into his shoulder. Pulling the hammer back gently, he tracked the Indian and squeezed the trigger.

The crash of the shot shattered the air. The Cheyenne grabbed the reins of his pony and hauled him violently back, then tumbled from the horse. The pony whinnied in confusion and, turning completely around, ran at the next Cheyenne, who was coming up fast. This Cheyenne swerved beautifully and kept coming. Reloading swiftly, Fargo sighted on him and fired. The .52-caliber slug smashed the Cheyenne in the head, disintegrating it. His pony kept going. The headless torso slumped forward, hung on to the pony for a few strides, then slipped to the ground.

Fargo shot two more Cheyenne off their horses before the war party wheeled and raced back to consider their options. As they pulled up better than three hundred yards back, Fargo loaded swifly and sighted on a Cheyenne whose back was to him. The warrior was punching the air with his fists, obviously urging his comrades to make another frontal attack. Fargo steadied the Sharps and took a deep breath. At three hundred yards, this would have to be one fine shot, Fargo realized, but not an impossible one for a Sharps. Properly handled, the Sharps could take the legs off a rattler at two hundred yards. Still holding his breath and lifting the barrel slightly, Fargo squeezed the trigger. A moment later, as the rifle's sharp crack died, the Cheyenne slipped from his pony.

Dismayed, the rest of the war party broke back. It was as if a lightning bolt had struck at them from out of a cloudless sky. A grim smile of satisfaction on his face, Fargo gathered up his remaining cartridges and hurried back to the pinto. Vaulting into his saddle, he headed deeper into the badlands. Already, the low sun was casting long shadows, turning canyons and arroyos into black, fathomless scars. But off to his right, Fargo saw a mile-long, narrow benchland looming above the badlands. On each side of it, the ground fell away almost straight down for at least forty to fifty feet. The benchland itself did not appear to be very wide, and it was covered with a thick pelt of dry, sun-baked grass.

He would like to think he had permanently discouraged the Cheyenne war party, but he did not allow himself that luxury. From the very beginning of this business, there had been some odd, unaccountable features—not the least of them that cavalry officer and his flashing saber. Accordingly, Fargo did not let up as he spurred his pinto toward the high benchland.

He was less than a quarter of a mile from it when he heard the Cheyenne once again boiling through the badlands after him. They were a determined bunch, that was for damn sure. Urging his now-lathered pinto to even greater speed, Fargo raced up onto the benchland and kept going.

When Fargo reached the far end of the shelf, he glanced back and saw the war party charging up onto the grassland. He watched them for a moment until all of them were on the benchland, sweeping toward him. Their cries grew more shrill when they saw him no longer racing away from them. They imagined him trapped, perhaps.

Off to Fargo's right there was a small piñon pine growing at the edge of the drop-off. He rode toward it, and pulling his pinto to a halt beside it, he dismounted and began kicking savagely at the base of the small pine. Snapping its thin trunk, he reached down and pulled on the broken portion, yanking the tree free of its roots. Crunching the branches under his boots, he took a match from his pocket and snapped it alight with his thumbnail. As it flared to life, he cupped the flame, then held it to the pine's dry needles.

Instantly, the tree crackled into life. Fargo whipped the tree back and forth to spread the fire through the branches. Then he touched the tree down. At once the grass caught. He paused a moment to watch and saw that the wind was just right. Already the flaming grasses were bending south, toward the onrushing Cheyenne.

Still holding the burning pine tree, Fargo leapt onto the back of his pinto. The terrified animal almost bolted. But Fargo managed to hold him, then rode off across the top of the benchland. As he rode, he leaned back and dragged the roaring torch through the tall grass behind him. Instantly, the wind caught the exploding grass and sent a long line of crackling flames sweeping back down the shelf toward the oncoming Cheyenne.

At the far side of the shelf, Fargo pulled the panicked horse to a sudden, hock-rattling halt and flung the torch from him. As he did so, he noticed that his buckskin sleeve was smoking, ready to flare up at any moment. He rubbed the sleeve hard against his pants leg, and giving the pinto his head, he put the animal off the shelf and into the rugged foothills beyond. He did not have to urge the Ovaro to hurry; the roaring fire at its back was more than enough incentive.

On a ridge well into the foothills, Fargo pulled up and looked back.

With the sun now below the horizon, a gloomy twilight covered the entire benchland, and what Fargo saw before him was a spectacular vision of hell. The grass fire sweeping back along the shelf, building momentum as it went. Occasional tongues of flame leapt high into the air. Black tendrils of smoke lifted from the ground, obscuring many of the fleeing Cheyenne, who by now were in full flight before this onrushing juggernaut of flame and smoke.

As Fargo watched, he saw a horse and rider pulled down from behind by a vaulting tongue of flame. The horse leapt and spun in its fiery grasp, its rider tumbling to the ground. The Cheyenne managed somehow to escape the flames, and Fargo could see him racing into the clear. But he went only a few feet before he stumbled and sprawled headlong. A moment later the flames swept over him. Another Cheyenne was overtaken, and then another. Some riders were able to leap clear of the flames, but others went down with their ponies, the blazing line of fire sweeping remorselessly on over their charred remains.

By this time the Cheyenne were beginning to realize they could not escape this fiery scimitar by outracing it, and they veered toward the edge of the shelf. Abandoning their ponies, they began clambering down the steep sides. Some lost their footing and went plunging out of sight; others were forced to hang for a while, then drop into the unknown blackness below them.

Through all this hell Fargo looked for that officer. But he did not see him. He watched a moment longer, then turned his pinto and continued on into the foothills, soon putting the benchland well behind him. Glancing back periodically, he caught sight of the smoke from the fire blotting out the stars, the still-blazing benchland sending an eerie glow into the sky.

By this time, Fargo should have relaxed. But he could not do so. He kept remembering that he had not seen that fool cavalry officer on the shelf. Perhaps the son of a bitch had urged the Cheyenne to split up before reaching it. If this were so, those

Cheyenne who had not raced onto the shelf would soon be closing in on him.

Fargo pushed on over the moonlit landscape, doing what he could to conserve the pinto, but keeping on relentlessly.

An hour or so later, Fargo heard the Cheyenne coming after him once more. He was at the far end of a rocky plain when he heard the distant thudding of unshod hooves on stone. Directing the pinto in behind a slab of black rock that towered into the night sky, he dismounted, snaked his Sharps from its scabbard, and climbed into the rocks until he was high enough to see them.

Their naked torsos gleaming in the moonlight, they streamed out onto the plain, then cut slightly to the left. By the time they had crossed the flat, they were out of sight, following a course through the badlands that paralleled Fargo's. Waiting a decent interval, until the faint sound of their passage had faded completely, Fargo moved back down the slope. Mounting up, he turned his horse away from the course the Indians had taken, passing through a stretch of boulder-strewn gullies and arroyos, doing his best to put as much distance as possible from the Cheyenne war party.

As he rode over the treacherous landscape, he tried to make sense of the events of the past three hours. These Cheyenne should long since have given up on him. He was a lone white man who had already caused them to lose too many braves. As Fargo knew from experience, though the redskin loved a fight, he lost his enthusiasm fast when he saw his losses piling up, for to them this meant the enemy's medicine was stronger than theirs. At such times the Indians felt it wise to retire to lick their wounds and hope for stronger medicine the next time. This was why they specialized in warfare that favored sneak attacks on feebly defended wagon trains, lone settlements, and defenseless women and children. The frontal attack was just too costly to a people not rich in manpower.

Why, then, since they had already lost so many braves tracking Fargo, were they still on his trail? And who in hell was this varmint with the sword? Was he a white savage who had gone over to the Indians or was he a Cheyenne who had scalped an officer, then taken his clothes and gear? And what kind of fool game was he playing, anyway?

Fargo pulled up. He heard unshod hooves coming toward him in the darkness. Swiftly, he pulled his pinto into an arroyo, splashed across a narrow stream, then moved in behind some scrub pine, and waited. After a short while, a small party of Cheyenne came into view, dismounted in the mouth of the arroyo, and proceeded to make camp, herding their ponies into the arroyo past the stand of scrub pine where Fargo crouched.

Soon they had a roaring fire going. A stocky brave stepped up to it and threw a haunch that looked as if it came from one of the dead horses onto the fire. They didn't let it get more than singed before the rest of them fell upon it and began slashing at it with their knives, devouring it greedily. Each brave stood out clearly in the light from the campfire. Fargo watched. The blood dripping from their mouths added a grisly touch to the already fierce daubings of war paint they wore.

Abruptly, a tall figure in a cavalry officer's uniform rode up. He was a captain, judging from the epaulets on his shoulder. The brim of his campaign hat was pulled well down over his forehead, preventing Fargo from getting a good look at his face—but it was a white face, and the captain favored a drooping wisp of a reddish mustache. Riding still closer, the captain swung his horse between Fargo and the camp-fire and began to berate the Indians in perfect Cheyenne. The Indians took the scolding docilely, their impassive faces looking up at the officer, their obsidian eyes gleaming in the firelight.

Fargo lifted his rifle. There were six Cheyenne in all, and Fargo calculated he could drop the officer with his Sharps; and if he was careful with the six remaining shots provided by his Colt, he could kill the remaining Cheyenne.

But Fargo's mother did not bring him up to die a fool. It was not likely the cavalryman or the Indians would stand quietly by while he finished them off so neatly. And the sound of gunfire would bring other Cheyenne, for it was now apparent that these bad-lands were swarming with Cheyenne, all of them under the command of this turncoat, this white sav-age in front of him.

Finished with his lecture, the captain spurred his horse and rode back the way he had come, moving off with a reckless speed, considering how treacher-ous the footing was in this dark, broken country. As soon as the captain vanished, the war party resumed their meal. The Cheyenne seemed a mite more sul-len than before, but no less enthusiastic about the singed horsemeat.

Fargo's pinto was well-trained and had not re-vealed its presence all this time, despite the proxim-ity of the Cheyenne ponies. But to make absolutely certain it did not betray Fargo's presence, Fargo slipped a rawhide noose around its mouth. He did not tighten the rawhide, but he kept it snug enough to let the pinto know what was expected of it. Shak-ing his head unhappily, the animal backed up and bobbed its head a couple of times. But that was the only protest it made as Fargo kept close, patting it soothingly.

Fargo settled down to wait.

The Cheyenne gorged themselves, then went to sleep. Fargo waited a while to make sure. Then he tied pieces of spare blanket over each of the pinto's hooves, tightened the rawhide about its mouth, and led the animal out from behind the pines. Moving so slowly and carefully that it took him nearly half an hour, he kept going up the arroyo until he was abreast of the Indians' ponies, who were feeding quietly on the other side of the stream.

At first he thought the ponies were unguarded, but as he stepped into the shallow stream, the ponies moved slightly and snorted almost inaudibly. He kept on across the stream, stepping slowly into the icy waters. Reaching the shore, he moved slowly into the ponies. They backed up, giving Fargo a glimpse of a shadowy figure sitting on the ground, his head bowed forward over his drawn-up knees. The Cheyenne had been sent to guard the ponies, but had gorged himself on horsemeat and been unable to stay awake.

Drawing his knife, Fargo rushed forward silently. As the ponies reared skittishly to get out of his way, the Indian came awake. His first glance, however, was straight ahead. By the time he turned his head and saw Fargo, it was too late as Fargo flung himself upon him, slamming his head back against a boulder. Before the Indian could cry out, Fargo had slit his throat. The Cheyenne's head lolled loosely back. Fargo jumped to his feet, but was not able to escape entirely the gout of blood that pulsed from the Indian's jugular.

Turning, he slashed the rope corral holding the ponies. Then he darted back to his pinto, ripped off the rawhide noose, and vaulted into the saddle. Letting out a blood-chilling yell that echoed sharply in the narrow arroyo, he sent the ponies charging madly down the arroyo ahead of him. Fargo rode with them, keeping his body low along the pinto's neck as the ponies boiled out of the arroyo. A few of the Indians tried to stop them, and a Cheyenne went down under one, screaming as he was trampled. The rest of the Indians scattered as the crazed ponies thundered on through their camp. Fargo turned his pinto and kept going.

He rode on for more than an hour without incident. At times he was forced to dismount and lead his horse off the trail in order to elude the small bands of Cheyenne riders combing the badlands for him. The dark landscape was as full of Cheyenne as a dog with fleas. At last he glimpsed ahead of him, just beyond a towering finger of rock, a long stretch of grassland. Under the clear light of the moon, it looked like a pale ocean. Fort Meade, he knew, should be less than ten miles farther on, and soon there would be ranches, even towns, places where a tired man could find rest.

Fargo spurred his Ovaro forward and was almost abreast of the tall rock when he caught a flick of movement in the rock's shadows. At the same time he felt something heavy bury itself in his side, just under his right arm. The pain was sudden and excruciating, but he forced himself to ignore it as he drew his Colt and thumb-cocking as fast as he could, he poured four rounds into the shadows. He heard the sound of a body thudding to the ground.

Looking down then, he saw the shaft of the Cheyenne arrow protruding from his side. It had gone in just under his rib cage. He decided against pulling it out. He had seen once the rush of blood that flowed out after an arrowhead was pulled free. Gritting his teeth, he snapped off the shaft, leaving the steel arrowhead still inside him.

Without looking back, he spurred on past the rock

and out onto the prairie. His head felt hollow and the stars dipped and spun about his head, but he kept going. He lost track of time. It felt as if he were drunk, but his mouth was too dry to shout at the moon, and his heart had no lightness in it, no joy.

He saw a window ahead of him, a light in it. Or was the window behind him? Confused, he halted the pinto too quickly and slipped from his saddle. He was amazed at how easy it was to fall. Coming to rest on his back, he looked dazedly up at the sky. It was growing lighter. The grass held him with a soft gentleness. The ground rocked slightly under him, transforming the earth into a cradle lulling him into a delicious sleep.

Only he mustn't sleep . . . he had things to do, women to meet he had not yet met . . . places to see he had not yet seen . . . and those men to track, the killers who had struck down his father. Yes, dammit! He had too much yet to do before he could take that long sleep.

He stirred himself and lifted his head. Though the arrowhead was still inside him, the grass under him was becoming slick and warm with his blood. Glancing up at the pinto, he saw the horse quietly cropping the lush grass at his feet. He reached up swiftly with his left hand and snatched the trailing reins, then hauled himself upright and leaned heavily against the pinto.

He could see the light from the ranch window clearly now. It was less than half a mile farther on. If he could reach it, they would have to take him in.

Waiting until he thought he could make it, he grabbed the pommel and hauled himself up onto the saddle, somehow managing to drag his right foot over the cantle. The pain that erupted from his side at this exertion caused him to groan audibly. The pinto looked back at him, its ears flicking questioningly.

Once secure in the saddle, Fargo took a deep breath and urged his horse toward the ranch house. He rode sagged over the saddle horn, the blood now pulsing out of his side, causing his right leg to grow heavier by the minute with the warm, encasing blood. He wondered crazily if the weight of the blood would be enough to drag him from the saddle.

He passed a large horse barn and two smaller sheds. The ribs of a corral stood out in the dim predawn light. He kept going until he reached the front of the ranch house. He got a vague impression of a long, low log structure with a pitched roof. The pinto pulled up abruptly. Fargo dismounted clumsily and started for the low veranda. He stumbled, reached out for the porch post, but missed. The next thing he knew he was on the ground again, staring back at the pinto.

The pinto pulled away from him, blowing nervously. Fargo tried to call out, but nothing came. He tried one more time, then felt himself sinking into the ground, into a deep, dreamless sleep.

JOIN THE *TRAILSMAN* READERS' PANEL

Help us bring you more of the books you like by filling out this survey and mailing it in today.

1. Book title:_____

   Book #:_____

2. Using the scale below how would you rate this book on the following features.

Poor		Not so Good			O.K.			Good		Excellent	
0	1	2	3	4	5	6	7	8	9	10

Rating

Overall opinion of book . . . . _____

Plot/Story . . . . _____

Setting/Location . . . . _____

Writing Style . . . . _____

Character Development . . . . _____

Conclusion/Ending . . . . _____

Scene on Front Cover . . . . _____

3. On average about how many western books do you buy for

   yourself each month?_____

4. How would you classify yourself as a reader of westerns?
   I am a ( ) light ( ) medium ( ) heavy reader.

5. What is your education?
   ( ) High School (or less)   ( ) 4 yrs. college
   ( ) 2 yrs. college   ( ) Post Graduate

6. Age_____   7. Sex: ( ) Male ( ) Female

Please Print Name_____

Address_____

City_____State_____Zip_____

Phone # (   )_____

Thank you. Please send to New American Library, Research Dept, 1633 Broadway, New York, NY 10019.

Wild Westerns by Warren T. Longtree